On the
Other Hand

On the Other Hand

June McCullough

iUniverse, Inc.
Bloomington

On the Other Hand

iUniverse books may be ordered through booksellers or by contacting:

iUniverse
1663 Liberty Drive
Bloomington, IN 47403
www.iuniverse.com
1-800-Authors (1-800-288-4677)

ISBN: 978-1-4502-9026-5 (sc)
ISBN: 978-1-4502-9027-2 (hc)
ISBN: 978-1-4502-9028-9 (ebk)

Library of Congress Control Number: 2011910498

Printed in the United States of America

iUniverse rev. date: 08/03/2011

In loving memory of my mother, Eva

Preface

In 1983, my mother passed away suddenly from a stroke at the young age of 59. Learning how to accept her death has been the most difficult thing I have ever had to do. My mother was always an inspiration to me and continues to be to this day.

Although I didn't write this book until recently, I believe that the premise for this book began with that event. I was convinced that God had made a mistake.

Being the analytical person that I am, I began to research medical books. I was determined to find what the doctors had missed, but it wasn't long before I had to admit that both life choices and genetics were factors in her death.

As painful as it was to lose my mother, it was just as difficult to watch my father as he struggled to understand how he could go into town for a few hours one morning and come home to find his wife of 38-years collapsed on the floor.

Since then, other family members and friends have lost spouses, and each time I am reminded of what my father went through. This is a compilation of their stories with a little of my own imagination added in.

If this is what you are going through now, or if you are watching someone you love go through this, I hope that through this book you will know that you are not alone.

If my mother were here today, she would say, "No matter how bad today is, there will always be a better tomorrow. I promise you." I heard her say those words more than once. And she was right; there was always a better tomorrow.

Love you, Mom.

Sunday, August 12

NINA SLOWLY STRETCHED IN AN attempt to bring herself out of a deep sleep and into what could at least be considered semiconsciousness. She raised her arms above her head, reached as far as she could while arching her back, and pointed her toes directly towards the doorway to the hall. With the stretch complete, she brought her arms down and rolled over to her side.

As she reached over to the other side of the bed, she realized that it had already been vacated; Mike was already awake and up. This discovery didn't surprise her. The cool sheets on his side of the bed had lost all warmth from his body heat, letting her know that he had been up for awhile.

In fact, she thought, he's probably already had his morning coffee and read the paper, which didn't surprise her either. For as long as she had known him, he had been an early riser, and during their 28-year marriage, he had always been the first one up—the only exception was when their children were young enough to require her presence and her presence alone.

Thoughts of the night before flashed through her memory, and she wondered if he was still upset with her. They had entertained a few people from his office, and she

1

had got a little tipsy—not drunk, just tipsy, but he hadn't approved of it. He had said he didn't think it was proper for the boss's wife to be anything but the gracious hostess in control of a wonderful evening.

Nina quickly tried to justify her actions in her own mind before she had to face him. Maybe it was because it had been a busy week, she reasoned, or it could be because she was tired. All she knew was that, for whatever reason, as she started visiting, telling stories, and listening to jokes their guests told, somewhere along the way she had forgotten her role of hostess.

She also refilled her wineglass a few more times than she had realized. Consequently, she had completely forgotten all about the hors d'oeuvres in the oven until they were burnt. Truth told, she hadn't remembered them even then. It was Mike who had taken them out of the oven and thrown them away. Try as she might, she could not remember what he had substituted them with. The one thing she did know was that she would never ask.

Rolling onto her back, she maneuvered her body into one more stretch. It wasn't until she relaxed from this position that she felt awake enough to even think about getting up. It also wasn't until then that she picked up the aroma of bacon and freshly brewed coffee.

She breathed in deeply to take in as much of the aroma as she could just as Mike entered the room carrying a large mug with steam rising above the rim, and she knew it was a cup of the morning mud, as he referred to it.

It was obvious to her that he was no longer upset with her, but then, that didn't surprise her anymore than finding him already up and busy.

"Good morning, Sleepyhead," he greeted her cheerfully. "Or is that Balloonhead? Thought you might need a little something to help deflate it a little."

Okay, so he wasn't mad, but he wasn't going to let it drop just yet either.

"My head is just fine, thank you very much," she replied, propping herself up on the pillow into a position that would allow her to drink her coffee without spilling it.

Nina was pleased when she realized that her headache could have been a lot worse. It didn't hurt too badly, but as soon as he left the room, she had every intention of sneaking into their en suite and taking two Tylenol with her coffee, just to take the edge off.

As he handed her the coffee, he leaned over and gave her a quick kiss on the lips and sat on the edge of the bed.

"Last night went pretty well, don't you think?" he said, rubbing her leg.

Nina held the mug to her lips and blew into it before taking a sip. "Actually," she said as she lowered the cup, holding it close to her chest, "I think it went very well, and I think everyone enjoyed themselves. It was really good of the company to pay taxi fare both here and home again for everyone. That way nobody had to worry about drinking and driving, including the boss who hosted the party. I know you always worry when someone has a drink here and then drives when they leave."

"Well, I'd feel responsible if someone had an accident because I served them a drink."

"You worry too much, but I suppose I should be grateful because that's one of the reasons I never have to. You always do enough worrying for both of us."

"Well, if I don't start worrying about breakfast, the bacon will get cold," he said as he started to stand and head for the door. "Drink your coffee, and then get your lazy butt out of that bed and into the kitchen for breakfast. You'll need all the nourishment you can get if we're going to get all the yard work done that we've talked about."

When Mike reached the doorway Nina called his name. "Mike?"

He stopped and turned to face her.

"I really am sorry about last night," she said, meaning it. "I should have watched how much I was drinking, and I guess I just got a little carried away."

"Don't worry about it," he replied. "You weren't the only one that might have tossed back a few more than they realized. I think a few people will be moving a little slower today, although I don't think anyone actually got drunk. Well, except Castles—he really got carried away, and it would serve him right if he couldn't get out of bed at all today."

With that comment he was out the door, and Nina was alone with her coffee. Setting it on the nightstand, she tiptoed into their en suite to get the Tylenol from the medicine cabinet.

It was a beautiful day without a cloud in the sky. The sun was shining, and the weatherman had promised that the temperature would reach 32°C by mid-afternoon. Both Mike and Nina wanted to get as much work done as possible before then.

After a full breakfast of bacon, eggs, diced potatoes, and sliced tomatoes, they sat on the deck at the back of the house drinking their coffee and quietly enjoying each other's company.

When the coffee was consumed, Mike headed for the garage to get the tools needed for the task at hand, and Nina carried the mugs back into the house to be washed with the rest of the dishes.

He made the breakfast, so she was responsible for the cleanup. It was an arrangement they had agreed to years before. Whoever did the cooking was not expected to do any of the cleanup. As a rule, he cooked breakfast and she usually prepared supper. This suited her just fine because it allowed her to sleep in longer, and she only had one or two pans to wash, putting the rest of the dishes in the dishwasher. It also meant that once they sat down for supper, her work for the day was finished.

As she stood by the sink, she thought again of how quickly he got over things. He was generally easy-going with the choices she made. Thinking back, she recalled the time he was totally forgiving of the $800 she spent for a picture without discussing it with him first because she saw it and just knew she had to have it. He never complained and was always a wonderful host, even if it had been a grueling week at work and all he wanted was to vegetate on the couch Friday night, only to find out that she had invited another couple over for a game of cards that evening.

None of this seemed to faze him. The only thing he ever asked was that she behave in a manner that he believed to be appropriate when they were around the people with whom he worked, and normally she was very good at allowing him this one request—but she did admittedly get a little carried away last night. And yet, to him last night was history. He had said whatever it was he had to say after the guests left, and now it was forgotten.

That was one of the few differences between them—one that always left Nina baffled. She knew darn well that if their shoes were reversed right now, she would have mentioned it last night, again this morning, and probably later again today. Without a doubt, she would have a two-day pout. In all their years together, she could never understand how he got over things so quickly. She only knew that he did and that she was grateful for it.

By the time she put away the last dish, she had decided that she would be especially nice to Mike today. She always appreciated him, but every now and then, she would make a point of going out of her way to let him know. In fact, she thought, I'm going to get two of the biggest, juiciest steaks I can find and serve them barbecued, with baked potatoes, corn on the cob, a salad, and a bottle of very expensive red wine.

With the cleanup complete, Nina wiped her hands on the dishtowel, hung it up, and made her way to the backyard. She was surprised when she didn't find Mike already staining the back fence. She walked around to the front and checked the garage. When she didn't find him there, she returned to the backyard. The yard isn't that big, she thought. How do you lose a husband in an area this small?

This time she called his name in case she had missed him, which seemed impossible, but she figured she'd give it a try. When he didn't answer, she wondered if he had gone over to the neighbours to borrow something. She decided to call one more time and then get on with her own chores. If he was next door, he'd be back soon. Besides, she reasoned, if I've got some of my own chores done before he gets back, maybe I'll win some brownie points to make up for last night.

She had just called his name a second time when she thought she heard a noise. Standing perfectly still, she listened for it again. When she heard the sound a second time, she realized it was coming from the side of the house. It almost sounded like a wounded animal, and she contemplated leaving until she could find Mike. Instead, she moved slowly towards the sound and tentatively called his name again.

"Mike? Is that you?" she asked, slowly moving forward. "Honey, are you there?"

As she cautiously approached the area, she wasn't sure what to expect, but never in her wildest dreams would she have guessed what she actually found as she turned the corner to the side of the house. There was Mike, balancing himself on his knees and elbows and holding his head in his hands.

Running towards him, she screamed, "Mike! What's wrong?"

"Oh, God . . . Nina . . . the pain."

She knelt down beside him. It was obvious that the pain was so terrible that it was making it difficult for him to speak. It was taking everything in him to get his words out, even one word at a time.

The look on his face was one that Nina recognized immediately, even though she had only seen it once before. A few years earlier, Nina and Mike had been out for an afternoon drive when they came across an accident that had happened just minutes before. The driver of the car had been travelling much too fast for the icy condition of the roads and slid sideways into a pole. He was killed instantly, but his female passenger was still alive and conscious. She was in a lot of pain, and as she cried out, Nina was reminded of a wounded animal in the woods. Shortly after they arrived, the passenger mercifully passed out, allowing her to escape the suffering. Mike had the same look on his face now that the passenger of the vehicle had had on her face then.

Nina noticed the vomit on the ground next to Mike. Not knowing what had happened, she shook with fear for her husband and knew instinctively that he needed more help than she could provide.

"Mike, honey," she said as she forced herself to stay calm enough to handle the situation. What should she do? "I'm going for help." She couldn't get out more than a short sentence at a time. "I'll be right back."

Nina stood and ran to get the phone. As small as the yard had seemed to her just minutes before, it now seemed too big for her to get to the kitchen quickly enough. Once in the house, she grabbed the cordless phone from the kitchen table and dialed 911. By the time a voice came on the other end, she was heading back out the door to let Mike know she was getting help.

"Please," she began with her voice shaking both from fear and from the motion of running across the yard as she spoke. "My husband is in a lot of pain. I don't know what's wrong. We need help."

Just then, Nina turned the corner to where she had left Mike and screamed. He was no longer on his knees, but lying on the ground motionless, his eyes closed.

"Oh my God," she screamed. "No, no!" She knelt down beside him, dropping the phone to the ground. "Mike! Mike! Oh my God, Mike!"

Just then she heard a voice in the background and remembered the 911 operator. Reaching over to where the phone had landed, she picked it up.

"Please, something's wrong. Please come right away. Please," she begged.

Later, Nina would have no memory of the dialogue between her and the woman on the other end of the line. She also had no idea how long it took for anyone to get there. Although the ambulance pulled into their driveway in a matter of minutes, in her mind it took too long, and she was sure they were lost.

Two men entered the backyard just as the voice on the other end of the phone told her, "They should be there." After a short pause, when Nina didn't answer, the voice said, "Ma'am, are they there?"

"Yes, thank you," she answered, disconnecting the phone as she ran to meet the paramedics to show them the way.

Nina stood back as the two men placed their bag on the ground next to Mike and began their work. She stood back to give them room. Craning her neck to see past them, she was looking for any sign of life from Mike. She was so absorbed on the scene in front of her that she hadn't noticed her neighbour, Scott, enter the yard or approach her. When he spoke, the sound of his voice startled her.

"What's going on?" he asked as he placed a hand on her shoulder. "I saw the ambulance drive up and thought I'd come over to see if I could help."

Trying to focus on what was happening, Nina looked up at him, taking a second to speak. "I don't know what happened, Scott. I just came out here and found him. I don't know what's wrong." None of this seemed real.

Just then one of the paramedics left the backyard while the other came over to where Nina and Scott stood. Facing Nina, he asked, "What is your husband's name?"

"Mike. Mike Andrews," she answered softly, her voice barely audible.

"My partner is getting the stretcher, and we're taking Mike to the hospital, Mrs. Andrews. Is he on any medication?"

"No," she whispered, finding it hard to speak.

"Does he have any medical problems?"

"No."

He asked a few more questions before his partner returned, and they quickly got to the business of getting Mike into the ambulance and transferring him to the hospital.

"Please," Nina asked, "what's wrong with him?"

The same paramedic who spoke with her earlier answered. Although he had a pretty good idea, it was not his place to say. "We won't know for sure until we get him to the hospital where they can run some tests." He turned to Scott. "I take it that you're a friend of theirs. Are you going to stay with her?"

"I'm going to the hospital with you. I'm not staying here." It was the first time since finding Mike that Nina's voice was strong, almost defiant. She wasn't about to stay and wait until they decided to phone her and tell her any news. She was going to the hospital in the ambulance with them, and she would stay there until she had answers.

"I'm sorry, but you can't ride in the ambulance with us, and I don't think you should drive." Once again he turned to Scott. "Can you drive her?"

"Of course."

At that, the paramedic turned to join his partner as they hurried Mike into the ambulance and drove away, lights flashing and siren blaring. Scott clearly saw the shock that Nina was in and put his arm around her shoulders, both to help calm her and to stop her from running after the ambulance. Two minutes later, Nina had locked up the house and was clutching her purse as she sat in the front seat of Scott's car sandwiched between him and his wife, Carrie.

While Scott skillfully wove between the cars of the traffic to get them to the hospital in record time, Carrie held Nina's cold, trembling hands in her own.

Grasping at any chance of hope, in a voice so quiet that Carrie had to strain her ears to hear, Nina said, "I've always hated the sound of ambulance sirens, but it's really a good sign, isn't it? It means they're getting him to the hospital as soon as they can so they can help him, aren't they? I mean, if . . . if . . ." At that her voice began to quiver, but she was determined to ask the question. Nina wiped away her tears, did her best to gain her composure, and asked, "If he were . . . you know . . . if it was too late, they wouldn't need the sirens, would they?"

"You're right, Nina," Scott replied, "The siren means that there is hope."

Scott stopped the car in front of the emergency entrance doors to let his passengers out before parking the car, and Nina wished she wasn't sitting in the middle. There was no way to get out without Carrie getting out first, and Carrie wasn't moving fast enough to satisfy her. Nina started moving towards the door, pressing against Carrie as she did. When Carrie finally did step out of the car, Nina was through the hospital doors and running towards the front desk before Carrie had time to shut the car door.

"My husband, Mike Andrews, was just brought in here," she started before even reaching the counter. "Can you tell me where he is?"

By this time, Carrie had caught up and was beside her. A woman a few years older than her entered the reception area at the same time. Elsa Brown was the head nurse in charge of the emergency room, and she was just coming back from looking after the last patient who had been brought into the examining room.

Elsa turned to the front-desk admitter and said, "It's okay, Louise, I'll look after this."

Anxious to know what was happening to Mike, Nina was oblivious to everything else going on around her. She didn't notice the dozen people sitting in the waiting room that were either waiting to get in to see a doctor or waiting for an update on their loved ones.

Ignoring her pounding heart and the fear that she was feeling, she made every attempt to appear calm as she repeated her question. "My husband, Mike Andrews, was just brought in here a little while ago. Can you tell me where he is?"

In a calm tone, Elsa Brown replied, "Mrs. Andrews, they are just getting your husband settled now, and the doctor will be out to speak with you when he has completed his examination. In the meantime, we need you to fill out some forms for us."

Nina fought the temptation to run back to the examining room and find Mike as the head nurse reached for a pen and a clipboard holding a sheet of paper with a list of questions. She then allowed herself to be guided to the empty chairs on the far side of the room. When she and Carrie were seated, she took the clipboard that the head nurse handed her and placed it on her lap.

As she stared at the paper, her eyes began to fill with tears, and the printing blurred, making it impossible to read. Holding the clipboard with one hand, she used the other to wipe the tears away. She was struggling to get control when she felt someone place a hand over hers.

"Have they told you anything yet?" Scott asked.

Nina looked up from the clipboard, and only then did she remember how she got to the hospital. As she slowly shook her head, Carrie answered for her. "They're looking at him right now. They said they'd be back to talk to us when they knew something."

"We're supposed to fill this out," Nina whispered as she lifted the pen to start. "Name. Michael Andrews." She read the question aloud, but the words never came out any louder than a hoarse whisper, and her hand shook so badly she couldn't hold the pen to the paper.

Carrie reached over, taking the pen and clipboard from Nina's grasp. "Why don't you tell me the answers, and I'll write them down?" The three of them sat there, Nina whispering the answers, Carrie writing them down, and Scott kneeling before the two of them, holding Nina's hand in an attempt to bring some calmness to her.

When Nina returned the clipboard to the front desk, she asked if she could speak with the doctor yet.

"I'm sorry, Mrs. Andrews. It's going to be a little while longer before they finish their evaluation. Dr. Hanson is with him right now."

"I can't sit here any longer. Do you know if I have time to go outside for a cigarette?"

"You go right ahead. If Dr. Hanson comes out, I'll let him know where you are."

"He won't think I've left, will he?"

"No. I know where you are and I'll be sure to let him know. I promise."

Nina walked back to Carrie and Scott. Just as she thought she would break down, she took a gasp of air and got some control of herself again.

"I'm just going outside for a cigarette."

Scott and Carrie stood up at the same time. "A little fresh air sounds good; mind if we join you?" Scott asked. Nina just shook her head, said nothing, and turned to leave.

The three of them stood to the side of the doorway, and Nina lit her cigarette. She was unable to stand still and started to pace. Subconsciously, her walk took on a pattern: she walked five steps away from her two companions, turned, and walked back.

"I don't know what happened," she said. "What if he fell off the ladder? I should have been there to hold it."

Five steps away, five steps back.

"I wonder why they're taking so long. They should know something by now."

Again five steps away, five steps back.

"What will I do if something happens? I mean... What..." She rubbed her forehead and tried desperately to make sense of what was happening.

"I wonder if I should phone the kids."

Then finally she said, "I can't wait anymore." With that, she stomped her cigarette butt into the ashtray and marched back into the waiting room. She was going to either get some answers or, at the very least, see Mike.

As she stepped through the doors, she heard her name. She turned towards the voice and saw the same nurse who had given her the clipboard earlier.

"I was just coming out to find you. Dr. Hanson is ready to talk to you now."

"Thank you," Nina replied. Still a little shaky, her voice was somewhat stronger than it had been earlier. "Can my friends come in?"

Nina had no way of knowing that the normal procedure of this hospital was immediate family only and that they were making an exception so she would not be alone when the doctor gave her the news.

"Certainly," she replied.

Nina expected to be taken to Mike's room, but instead she was led to a small room with a couch, a couple of chairs, and a coffee table with a few magazines on it. After escorting them to the room, Elsa Brown left, closing the door behind her.

The three had just sat down when the door opened again, and a tall, gray-haired gentleman entered. Nina guessed from the white jacket and stethoscope that this was Dr. Hanson.

All three stood as the man standing at the doorway spoke. "Mrs. Andrews?" he asked as he looked straight at Nina.

Nina watched him approach. The fear and apprehension were etched on her face like a second skin. Though she wanted desperately to be told what had happened to Mike, she was afraid of what it was that she would hear.

Nina stood watching him, every step bringing him closer. Her breath caught in her throat; it was the breath of anticipation. When he reached her, he held her hands in his and sat her down on the couch.

"Mrs. Andrews, your husband has had a stroke." He paused just long enough for her to realize what he had just said. As she looked at him in disbelief, he continued. "He is in a coma right now, and we have him on life support. If there are any other family members, it might be a good idea to call them."

For the next two days, Nina never left Mike's side for more than a couple minutes. Scott and Carrie had offered to phone the kids for her, but she had insisted on doing this herself. She dreaded making the calls almost as much as she dreaded being in this place. What should she tell them, that their father was going to die, and if they wanted to see him one more time, they had better hurry home? Or that he was in critical condition, but there was always hope. She chose the latter, because she knew she wasn't ready to believe there was no hope. There always had to be hope.

Both of the kids lived within a three-hour drive. Mark, their son, worked for a bank and insisted on coming down to be with her right away. He would phone his supervisor in the morning from her place and explain the situation. Jan, their daughter, was a teacher and couldn't drive down until the next morning. She would need to arrange for a substitute teacher and make sure the school had her assignments and class plans for the next week.

Neither Mark nor Jan could get Nina to leave the hospital, so they stayed with her in shifts. When they weren't there, they were at the house they had grown up in, or they were running errands for their mother.

It didn't matter what anyone said to her; Nina would not leave Mike's side for more than a few minutes at a time. The hospital had assured her repeatedly that they would call if there was any change. When they realized that there was no way she was going to leave, they set up a cot for her. The little sleep she did get was by her husband's side.

Mike and Nina had been together for more than half her life. They had been through a lot in that time, and never once had one of them left the other alone to deal with a difficult situation. They were a team, and she wasn't about to leave him now. She knew that if he woke up, she wanted to be there for him and she wanted to be the first person he saw. If her worst nightmare came true . . . well, she wanted to be there for him then too.

Nina had been at the hospital for 52 hours and 18 minutes when it happened. He never did come out of the coma. Late Tuesday afternoon, he just slipped away.

Her memory of the events that she did remember over the past few days came to her in pieces. Nothing flowed together. She couldn't remember Jan or Mark arriving; she could only remember that they weren't there, and then they were. She didn't remember Scott and Carrie leaving the hospital, but she knew from Jan that they had. She wasn't sure what day it was. It felt like one long day that had stretched to eternity, and at the same time, it felt like it was over all too soon.

As long as she was living in the nightmare of the past few days, at least she still had Mike in her life. There was still hope. But now he had been taken from her, and she knew her nightmare was about to get worse.

It was Jan's shift when it happened; Mark was at home trying to catch a little sleep. The women held each other close as they wept together.

Suddenly Nina pulled her shoulders back, held her chin high, and took a step back. Looking at her daughter with quiet strength, she said, "We need to tell your brother."

The past few days had been a haze for her, and there was very little that she could remember since that Sunday morning, but, as she left the hospital, she knew that for some reason, 52 hours and 18 minutes was an important fact not to be forgotten.

Friday, August 17

PAT MCDERMOTT PLACED THE PHONE receiver back in its cradle, turned, and stared out her office window. She was still trying to digest the news that she had just received. She wished she'd had the luxury of reading the newspaper at home the night before. The news would still have come as a surprise, but it would have been easier for her to gather her thoughts before having to speak to anyone.

Her usual evening routine included having a quiet cup of coffee over the local newspaper after getting the kids into bed. Given her usual routine, she wouldn't have had to find out this way, but her schedule had been hectic this week, more hectic than normal. Between trying to juggle meetings for work and with her divorce lawyer, plus running the kids to appointments with the doctor, and shopping for new clothes before school started in a few weeks, she had little time for anything else. The little time she did have was taken up arguing with her soon-to-be ex-husband. There just had not been enough time or energy to sit and read the evening paper, which meant that she had not read the obituaries either.

Pat was a financial planner and over the past 15 years, she had built up a clientele that was large enough and profitable enough to provide her with a very healthy income. All her new business now came from referrals, and there was no longer a need for the cold calls she had to do when she first started out.

In the beginning, she had worked long, hard days. She could still remember months when, had it not been for the money she inherited from her grandmother, she would not have been able to pay the rent. Pat had always been grateful for the money left to her and believed that without it, she would have been forced into a more stable—and in her opinion, boring—career.

Never one to give up, she had struggled through the first few years, working from seven in the morning until ten at night. She would follow every lead and kept meticulous notes on every contact. She knew the names of every family member, where they had vacationed, and what sports the children played. Every time she called, she would ask about these things the way a friend would. Before long, the contacts trusted her and invited her over for the evening to discuss their finances. The first time Pat visited their homes, she was visiting the home of a potential client. With few exceptions, the first time Pat left their homes, she left the home of a client.

Her list of clients slowly grew, and now among her colleagues, her name was synonymous with success; and she was a mentor to many of the new financial planners.

To her surprise, her success also provided her with an unexpected supplementary income as an inspirational speaker. At first it was only the financial consulting firms that hired her to speak, but word got out of her enthusiastic approach and her ability to hold audiences' attention. After listening to her speak, the attendees left the room wanting to be the best that they could be in their field of expertise, and soon many businesses, including large oil companies, engineering firms, and retailers, were seeking her out in the hope that she would inspire their employees.

Pat never took her success for granted. Although she was able to admit to herself that it was her hard work and determination that brought her success, she always felt very fortunate to have the success that she did. She no longer had to worry where her next paycheque came from to keep from starving, but she vowed to never forget the days when the only thing between her and starving was just one more client.

That time in her life had been a struggle, and she had often wondered if she would be forced to choose another line of work. But she was never one to quit. When Pat McDermott took on a battle, she stayed the field until the battle was over. Win or lose, she always walked away knowing that she had given it her all.

Pat was proud of what she had accomplished. She no longer made the initial contact with the client; they contacted her after being referred, which is how she had first met Mike and Nina Andrews. Friends of theirs were clients of hers, and when Mike and Nina had expressed dissatisfaction with their current financial planner, their friends had suggested calling Pat.

That was two years ago, and she had been working with the Andrews ever since. From their first meeting, she had envied their relationship. The love and friendship they shared was obvious, and with the recent failure of her own marriage, she envied them even more.

She had an appointment with Mike and Nina Andrews to review their financial plan tomorrow morning at ten o'clock. As always, she personally phoned the day before the meeting to confirm. When she called the Andrews' home this time, a young woman answered.

"Hello?"

"Nina?"

"No, this is her daughter, Jan Andrews."

"Oh, Jan. This is Pat McDermott. I don't believe we've met, but your parents speak of you often. You're a teacher, right?"

"Yes."

"When did you get down?"

"Monday."

Okay, Pat thought, given the one-word responses, it appears that conversation with Jan isn't going to happen. Pat had learned years ago not to take this personally and assumed that the other person had something on her mind. It was best to keep these connections short and to the point.

"May I speak with your mother, please?"

"I'm sorry; she's not taking any calls. Can I help you?"

Their meeting was set up for Saturday morning because Mike worked Monday to Friday, so Pat knew there was probably no point asking for him.

"I have an appointment with your parents tomorrow morning, and I'm just phoning to confirm. Do you know if tomorrow morning at ten o'clock is still a good time, or should I call back and talk to one of them later?"

"I'm sorry we never called you. I thought we had called everyone we needed to advise."

There was a slight pause as Jan apparently gathered her strength. "My father passed away on Tuesday. The funeral is today."

Pat's grip on the receiver tightened in her hand, her jaw dropped, and she remained speechless. It took a few seconds before Pat was finally able to form any words. "I'm so sorry. I've known your parents for two years now." Even as she said it, she wondered why she had felt the need to offer that piece of information. It probably didn't matter to this girl how long Pat had known her parents.

This was not Pat's first client to die, but this was the first time she had found out while a family member was on the other end of the line. Every other time, the client had either been sick for awhile, or she had at least read it in the obituaries first. She'd always had time to think of what she would say, but this time, she had been caught totally off guard.

"I'm sorry. I...I don't know what to say," she stammered.

At that point, Pat felt herself becoming emotional, and knew she had to hang up before she lost her professionalism. "Please, tell your mother that I am so sorry." Another small pause. "I'll call her in a couple days." Trying to keep a businesslike tone, she added, "There are a few things I will need to go over with her."

Pat was still staring out the window when she heard her assistant, Nancy, call her name from the doorway.

Nancy had worked for Pat for five years, and during that time, their association had grown beyond employer and employee. The two were close in age, but that was where the similarities ended. The difference in their personalities was as obvious as the difference in their appearances. Pat was a petite brunette with a flair for fashion. She always looked the part of a businesswoman and had a presence that demanded respect and confidence. Her clothes were invariably the most up-to-date, her hair stylishly combed and her makeup perfect.

She had an extremely busy social life, although that had slowed down significantly since becoming a single mom. Her son, Nathan, was 8 and her daughter, Chelsea, was 6. The most important task in Pat's life these days was to make sure her children came out of this divorce as unscathed as possible.

The divorce was not yet final, but Pat and Jack had separated 19 months earlier. In the beginning they had been able to be civil with one another, but it seemed like the closer the divorce came to being final, the more tension there was between them. Lately they couldn't spend more than five minutes together before the bickering began.

Nancy, on the other hand, was considered tall at five feet ten and a half inches, and according to Pat, she was 15 pounds underweight. Her hair was worn straight to the shoulders, she only wore makeup on special occasions, and her wardrobe consisted of outfits that, at best, would be called nondescriptive. She was uncomfortable when people directed attention towards her, so she always tried to blend in.

A few months earlier at a luncheon that both women had attended, Pat had realized just how successful Nancy had become at blending in. The two had agreed to meet, and Pat had looked around the room several times before spotting Nancy not more than 10 feet away from her. Deciding that Nancy blended in too well, Pat had attempted to update her assistant's style a bit, but Nancy would have no part of it.

Pat had been married 10 years before the marriage fell apart, whereas she could only remember Nancy having half a dozen dates, at most, in the five years the two women had known each other. In business, Pat was the boss and Nancy the assistant; on a personal level, Pat had subconsciously accepted the role of mentor. During the past six months, though, as Pat's separation from Jack turned into a divorce proceeding, it was Nancy who handed out the personal advice and Pat who listened.

Pat didn't respond when her name was called, so Nancy called again, a little louder. "Pat?" Pat turned to face her with tears in her eyes.

"Pat, are you okay? Is it that bastard husband of yours again? Why do you talk to him? Tell him to talk to you through your lawyer."

"Bastard" was extremely strong language for Nancy, and normally it would have made Pat smile just to hear the word come from her assistant's lips, but today she didn't even notice.

"No, it's not Jack."

She moved closer to her desk, sighed, cupped her chin into her hands, and looked over to her assistant.

"I just found out that a client of mine died on Tuesday. Michael Andrews. I really liked him too. I don't know if I feel worse for him because his life is over at 51, or for his wife because of her loss. At least I chose not to be with my husband—she wasn't given a choice."

Pat leaned back in her chair. "Do we have this morning's paper in the office? I need to know which funeral home to send the flowers."

"Let me check. If not, I'll run out and get you one. Do you want me to pull the file and start the paperwork?"

"Yes, please," Pat answered softly as she slowly turned her chair back to face the window, letting Nancy know that it was time for her to take her leave.

~ ~ ~ ~ ~ ~ ~ ~ ~ ~ ~ ~ ~ ~ ~ ~ ~ ~ ~ ~

At two o'clock that afternoon, the limousine provided by the funeral home pulled up in front of the Andrews' home to pick up Nina and her children. The use of the vehicle was available to them all day to take them to the services, the graveside, the reception that was to follow, and home again.

Both Mark and Jan were worried about their mother. It appeared to them that she had barely been hanging on all week. She insisted on being a part of every decision but refused to talk to anyone except Mark or Jan. She rarely ate and often cried. They both thought that today would be the most difficult for her, with the funeral and a room full of people. They weren't sure what to expect, especially if she didn't take her prescription.

Mark had met with their family doctor earlier in the week and got a prescription for a mild sedative for his mother. As far as they could tell, she'd had a total of about ten hours sleep during the entire week. Each night, after their mother had gone to bed, Mark and Jan stayed up for an hour to make sure she was settled and didn't need anything. This gave them time to talk alone, and hopefully it gave their mother enough time to fall asleep.

Every night, lying in their own beds afterwards, they prayed for sleep to come soon so they would have the strength to get through the madness they knew the next day would bring. The first night they came home from the hospital, all three went to bed exhausted. After settling in, Mark and Jan lay in their beds, staring at the ceiling, thinking through the events of the past couple days when they each heard the noise. They came out of their rooms at the same time and stood in their doorways listening. Together they had followed the noise, slowly stepping down the hallway.

In the living room, they found their mother, alone and crying in the big armchair in the corner. Not wanting to disturb her children, she had buried her face in a throw pillow. They knew there were no words to comfort her. All they could do was hold her in their arms as she had done for them so many times all those years ago.

Now, it was the day of the funeral. Nina had refused to take any of the sedatives all week, but she had been shaking so badly 15 minutes before the limousine arrived that Mark and Jan had argued with her until she had finally agreed. They both knew that without the medication, there was no way their mother would have made it through the day.

Sitting in the limousine now, Jan watched her mother. Nina sat staring out the side window, clutching onto her Kleenex. Her tears welled up but none fell, and Jan knew the pill was starting to take its effect. She looked over to her brother to see how he was holding out and saw his chin quiver. A tear escaped and fell down his cheek. She watched as he bit his lip and turned his gaze from their mother to her. Jan wiped the tear from his cheek and then turned to look out the window next to her. Each had their own thoughts; each had their own pain, but they all shared the same loss. No one spoke.

Neither Mark nor Jan really had any time to mourn yet. Both had agreed that, for now, their mother needed them. Their time to mourn would come later. Being the only two siblings, they were close and they had made a pact to help each other through this.

When they arrived at the funeral home, Nina, Jan, and Mark were escorted to the family room, away from the other mourners. The music that Nina had chosen could be heard in the background through the speakers. Slowly, the chapel filled with family and friends. When all the seats were occupied, employees of the funeral home brought chairs into a second room where the service would be heard through the intercom system.

When it was time for the service to begin, the family was led to the front row of the chapel. The song ended and the minister stood before them. He looked out over the people who had gathered before he began. "Acts 1:7 states, 'And he said unto them, *It is not for you to know the times or the seasons, which the Father hath put in his own power.*' We often talk of the seasons of our life, but only God knows what season we are truly in. Each season brings a new beauty and a new joy of its own, but just as the seasons of our world vary from year to year, so do the seasons of our lives vary from person to person."

Nina had never taken a sedative before and was surprised at the effect it had on her. She was able to make it through the service and graveside visit, aware of what was going on around her, but she somehow felt removed from her own surroundings. It all seemed so surreal. By the time she arrived for the reception, she was numb of all emotion.

Nina stood in the corner of the small room the family had rented for the reception, drinking her coffee, void of any thought or feeling. It's as if my body is here, but my insides have gone to sleep, she decided. After a week of high emotions, she was grateful for the numbness.

She looked around for Mark and Jan. When she realized that neither was by her side, she suddenly felt very vulnerable and unprotected. This was the first time one of her children was not next to her since they had arrived five days earlier. Panic started to set in when she spotted Jan across the room. She started to make her way over, only to be stopped every few feet by well-wishers.

Everyone who stopped her, from the people at Mike's office to her family and friends, seemed to think she should take comfort in the fact that he didn't suffer long. Nina knew they meant well, but at that moment, she wished they wouldn't say anything at all.

Maybe it's the sedative, she reasoned, but the things people are saying to me seem to be just ridiculous.

"Well, at least he never suffered," said one. "A lot of people go through a lot of pain and just hang on, making it difficult on everyone."

"He had a good life, Nina," said another. "You can take comfort in that."

Someone else proclaimed, "I know he loved you very much; you were everything to him."

Nina could not figure out why they insisted on looking for some good in this. There was no good. No, he didn't suffer a long time, but her life companion was gone. Yes, he had a good life, but that didn't mean it was okay that it was over. He didn't want to leave this life—it was not his choice. It was not her choice to be left alone. They had been very happy. What was she supposed to do now?

They had been married 28 years and together as a couple for two years before that. For more than half her life, he had been a part of it. Now, without any warning—when they were in the prime of their lives, when they were finally able to do all the things they had put off doing until the house was paid and the kids were grown, when they finally had enough time and money to do the things they had always planned—he had been taken. Nina refused to think of his death in any other way; he had been taken.

She wanted to scream at them all, "Don't tell me there is anything good in this, because there's not. There's nothing good about this."

Nina quit listening. One reason was because she chose not to, but the main reason was because she no longer had the strength.

Instead, she just stood there, nodding her head. As far as the speaker could tell, she was listening to every word. She let them talk but heard nothing, and when she realized that they were finished speaking, she would simply say, "We were at the hospital for 52 hours and 18 minutes. I don't really remember going there, and I don't remember coming home, but I remember that it was 52 hours and 18 minutes. I wonder why that seems so important to remember. Strange, don't you think?"

With that, she would turn and walk away.

Monday, August 20

THE AIR-CONDITIONING IN THE OFFICE was already a welcome relief at nine o'clock that morning, and Pat knew the day was going to be another scorcher. She looked at the file lying on the desk in front of her but made no attempt to open it. It had been a relaxing weekend, and she wasn't ready for it to be over.

Her appointment with Mike and Nina Andrews had been her only scheduled appointment of the weekend. When that was cancelled, it meant that she had two days free of any appointments or obligations, so she left the city Friday night with kids and dog in tow, and they had spent the weekend at her cabin.

Because the trip had not been in her plans, they got a late start. It was dark, and both kids were sound asleep in the back seat by the time they arrived at their destination. During the summer months, she always kept the cabin supplied with enough essentials for times like this. The only thing she needed to pick up on their way out of town was milk.

Anytime her life overwhelmed her and she found it difficult to deal with the issues at hand, Pat loaded the kids and the dog into the car and headed for the cabin. The peacefulness of sitting on the deck drinking a tall iced tea and reading a trashy romance novel, while Nathan and Chelsea fished off their dock, always brought a much-needed calm back to her life. It was during these weekends that she was able to escape her life, putting all thoughts of divorce, work, and death from her mind, even if for only a few minutes at a time. Pat relished those moments.

When she arrived back home Sunday night, the message light on her phone was blinking, reminding her that there was no way of avoiding the realities of her life forever. Wanting to escape for just a little while longer, she unpacked, bathed the kids, and put them to bed before playing the messages.

The first message was a pleasant surprise. "Hello, Pat. I'm not sure you remember me. This is Gordon Atkins. We met a couple times before I moved away two years ago, but I've moved back now—about three weeks ago. I don't know many people in town anymore, and I heard you were single again. I was hoping we could get together for dinner or a drink. I'll give you a call later in the week."

There was a pause in the message before Gordon continued. "I'm sorry. This message will probably sound really stupid when you hear it, but I hate these machines. I never know what to say. I spoke with Janine a few days ago, and she told me to call. Well, didn't exactly *tell* me to call, but when I mentioned it to her, she said she thought it would be a good idea. Anyway . . . I'll give you a call later in the week, and if you're not totally repelled by this message, maybe we can get together."

Pat stopped the tape and thought back. Gordon Atkins? A fuzzy vision came to her as she remembered a man she had first met at a party given by her best friend, Janine. If memory served her right, he was good-looking and had a quiet, friendly manner about him. They had bumped into each other a few times after that at different social functions, and then he just seemed to disappear. So that's what happened to him: he had moved away. Pat hadn't given him another thought until now. She made a mental note to give Janine a call the next day to get the scoop on this Gordon. Why hadn't Janine warned her that he might call?

Starting the tape player again, she recognized the voice from the next message right away. It was her soon-to-be ex-husband, Jack. "Pat, I tried to get you on Friday, but you had already left the office. I went over the latest divorce proposal with my lawyer and signed it. He wasn't too pleased and advised against it, but I figure we could go back and forth a couple more times with the negotiations, and nobody really wins—except maybe the lawyers. The settlement seems fair for both of us, and maybe if we stop our bickering now, we can at least get back enough of our relationship to get along for the kids' sake."

Pat stopped the player one more time as the tears formed. An amicable relationship with Jack was what she had wanted all along, but every conversation between the two of them lately made even the thought of it seem like an impossibility.

For Pat, the hardest part of the break-up was realizing that someone she had deeply loved and planned on spending the rest of her life with was now someone she couldn't spend more than five minutes with. Where had it all gone wrong? She'd been over the question a thousand times. The problem was neither of them, and at the same time it was both of them. She would contact her lawyer first thing tomorrow morning to sign the papers. Maybe now she could put this part of her life behind her.

She pressed the play button down one more time to listen to the last message and was surprised to hear Jack's voice come over the speaker again. "Listen . . . I don't know what you'll think of this. I was thinking and...well, we weren't all bad. I really do wish you all the best, Pat. I know I've been the cause of most of our disagreements lately. I guess I was still a little angry and maybe a little bitter. I really think I'm over that because I want you to be happy, and to be honest, up until this week I only wanted you to be miserable. I guess I did my best to make you miserable, too, didn't I? I'm sorry. Do you think we could get together for a drink this week and try to repair some of the damage—as friends, I mean? I know it probably sounds foolish to you, and I know that as a couple we screwed up, but maybe we could be friends."

There was a pause and Pat wondered if that was the end of the message when his voice came over the speaker again. "Well . . . give me a call if it sounds all right to you."

She quickly glanced at her watch and knew he would still be up. It was only 9:45. Whereas she had to be in bed within the next half-hour if she was going to be able to function at all tomorrow, she knew he would still be up for another three to four hours. Knowing his phone number by heart, she picked up the receiver and dialed.

Pat forced all thoughts of the weekend out of her mind. It was time to concentrate on the present. She picked up the file Nancy had placed on her desk earlier and studied it. She had only dealt with a couple of estates, but she knew that enough time had passed. Mike Andrews had died a week ago, and the funeral had been three days ago. The quicker she got this done, the better for both her and Nina Andrews.

Thinking she was going to get the answering machine, she was about to hang up on the fourth ring when a woman's voice came on the line. She recognized the voice from her last phone call.

"Jan?"

"Yes."

"Jan, this is Pat McDermott. How is your mother doing?"

"Better. I think she's sleeping more, even though she hasn't slept through the night yet. Thank you for the flowers; they were beautiful. Did you need to speak with my mother?"

"Actually, I was hoping to get together with her. Your father had life insurance through one of the agents I represent, and we need a few documents signed. I realize that it may seem awfully soon, but the sooner these details are taken care of, the better. Do you know if she's ready to meet with me?"

"Hang on, I'll ask."

Pat shuffled through the papers in the file that she had studied just minutes before as she waited for Jan to return to the phone. Instead of Jan's voice, it was a tired, lifeless voice that she heard next.

"Pat?"

"Nina, is that you?"

"Sorry I didn't speak with you sooner. Thank you for the flowers, they were beautiful."

There was no emotion behind the words and Pat was left with a vision of a robot from the movies Nathan loved to watch.

"Nina, if you're up to it, we should get together and go over some papers."

"There seems to be so many things that need handling. I don't know what I would have done without the kids. They've been a great help."

"How long are they there? Did you want me to come over before they leave?"

"Actually, Mark left yesterday so he could get some things done. He'll be back tomorrow, though, and he's staying until the end of the week. Jan is leaving tomorrow. Can we get together Wednesday, when Mark is here?"

"That would be fine. How's ten o'clock Wednesday morning?"

"Fine."

When Nina put the phone down, she turned to her daughter. "Pat's been helping us get . . ."

Nina's chin began to quiver, and she paused. "Well, I guess she'll be helping *me* make a new plan now. It seems a bit soon, don't you think?"

Jan walked over to the counter and reached for the coffee-pot. She had found it necessary to keep busy since her arrival. It was normally her mother who did so much for her whenever she came home to visit. This time it was Jan who did practically everything. But she was grateful for it; if she had too much time to think, the reality of it all would sink in, and she knew she wasn't ready to cope with any of it yet. If she let it sink in now, she knew she would be no help to her mother. There was always tomorrow after she went back to her own home and Mark was here.

"She probably doesn't want to go over your whole plan, Mom. Pat said something about life insurance. She probably just wants to go over that."

Jan hesitated before asking her next question. She didn't want to upset her mother, but she did want to be sure that her mother wouldn't have any unnecessary worries. "Mom, you'll be okay, won't you? Financially, I mean—now that you won't have Dad's paycheque?"

Since Mark and Jan had left home, Mike and Nina had helped them each financially on a couple occasions. If it was necessary to return the favour now, Jan knew that both she and Mark would do so willingly. Whatever their mother needed from them, neither one would hesitate to bestow it upon her.

Nina walked over and put her arm around her daughter, clearly recognizing the concern in her voice. "Oh, Baby, don't worry about me. Your father and I have been planning our finances for some time now. We wanted to be sure that we could enjoy our retirement and not be a burden to you or Mark. We thought we would look at retirement in five years." After a short hesitation, Nina continued. "Between our savings and the life insurance, I'll be able to do all the things we planned now. Ironic, isn't it?"

Nina clearly wanted to end the conversation, and she started walking towards the doorway. "I think maybe while that coffee is dripping, I'll start a load of laundry. There are some sandwiches in the fridge. Why don't we have them with the coffee? We can have lunch out on the deck."

Jan was pleased that her mother was eating again, even if it was just enough to keep a kitten alive. At least it was something. She also noticed that, little by little, her mother had been doing more around the house the past few days.

Although her mother was improving, Jan couldn't help but worry about next week, or the weeks that followed when Nina would be on her own. She knew that both she and Mark would phone often, but that wasn't going to be enough.

So often she had heard of family and friends giving their support and attention for the first few weeks . . . and then they got on with their own lives. The person in mourning was often left feeling even more alone.

During the past 10 days, there had been a lot of friends and neighbours dropping in. Each time, Jan or Mark had pulled them to the side asking each of them to look in on their mother, and each time they had promised they would. Jan and Mark only hoped that they were good to their word.

While placing the sandwiches on a tray, Jan heard the back door open and close. She knew it was her mother leaving the house to go to the backyard. A few minutes later Jan followed, carrying the tray holding sandwiches and coffee out to the deck. When Jan got to the back deck, there was no one in sight. Jan took a quick look around the backyard and wasn't surprised to see it empty. She knew exactly where to look.

The first time Jan and Mark couldn't find their mother, they were anxious. It wasn't long before they realized that any time they couldn't find her in the house, they would always find her at the side of the house where she had found her husband that fateful day. They could only imagine what she was thinking, but it seemed to them that she was reliving what she found when she came around the corner and found him on his hands and knees, crying out from the pain; then, after her frantic call to 911, when she found him lying unconscious beside his vomit.

Hearing the description of what her mother had witnessed that day, the first thing Jan had done after arriving at the house was to force herself to the spot where her mother now stood. She knew that of all the memories her mother had gathered over the years, the side yard would hold only one memory for her now. All the old memories had been replaced by the one memory of August 12.

Jan knew that she could never remove the memory, but she wanted to remove any physical evidence before her mother came home. Stepping around the corner of the house, with good intentions and hose in hand, she was surprised to find the area already cleaned. The mystery was cleared up when Scott and Carrie brought over a casserole later that day. When she asked them about it, they explained that they had the same thought and had cleaned the area the same day they drove Nina to the hospital.

Jan stood silently and watched her mother now, wishing she knew of some way to help ease the pain. Never in her life had Jan experienced the level of sadness that she had been experiencing since her father's death, but that sadness was no greater than her feeling of helplessness as she watched her mother try to just make it through another day. She couldn't imagine the pain her mother felt. She only knew that her mother believed that her own life had ended with his.

Not wanting to startle her, Jan stood back and quietly called her name. When there was no response, Jan moved a little closer and called again, this time a little louder. Nina slowly turned around as if in a daze.

"Yes, Dear?"

"Mom, I have our sandwiches and coffee ready."

"Oh, right," and with that Nina slowly made her way to the deck.

When they had eaten the sandwiches and were having their coffee, Nina pulled out her cigarette pack. Jan wanted to talk to her about quitting the habit; she was convinced that if her father hadn't smoked, he might still be alive today. She didn't want to think of the possibility of losing her only other parent. Instead, she silently sat and watched as Nina held the flame of her lighter to the cigarette, knowing that now was not the time to bring it up.

"This is the last place your father and I spoke. We'd just had breakfast and were having a coffee before getting to the yard work."

Nina told her this each time they sat on the deck, but Jan made a point of not reminding her. Instead the two women sat in silence, each with their own thoughts. The remainder of the day was uneventful, much the same way Nina saw the rest of her life.

Wednesday, August 22

ON WEDNESDAY MORNING, AT PRECISELY 10:00 a.m., Pat stopped her car in front of the Andrews' house. As she reached for her briefcase containing the file, a feeling of guilt came over her. At the same time her life was finally coming together and she was beginning to experience tranquility and contentment, Nina's life was falling apart.

Pat reflected on life for a moment and how quickly everything could change. It was only two weeks ago that Nina had been perfectly content and was totally oblivious to the fact that her life was about to change forever. Today, instead of sharing each day with her soul mate and planning for the future, she was alone and could no longer see a future.

Two weeks ago, Pat had been constantly battling with Jack, trying to come to an agreement so they could finalize the divorce, and there was definitely no prospect of a new love, let alone a date. Now, she and Jack had signed the divorce papers, she had a date with Gordon, and her future looked brighter.

With butterflies of anticipation in her stomach, Pat had met Jack for drinks the night before. Except for their telephone conversation two days earlier, their conversations since the separation could only be called civil, at best. This was the first time the two had sat down together since the night he moved out. She had been nervous and wasn't sure what to expect.

Looking around the dimly lit lounge, she first noticed Jack when he stood up to make his location apparent to her. He remained standing until she reached the table. As she sat, she noticed the two drinks.

"I hope you don't mind," he said while gesturing to her drink. "I took the liberty of ordering for you. You still drink Singapore Slings, don't you?"

Pat reached for the drink and brought it to her lips. It was not what she had planned on ordering, and a flood of emotions washed over her. This had been one of their problems: he always took the liberty of making decisions.

In the beginning, the decisions had only been small ones, like knowing what she drank and ordering for her. At first, it thrilled her that he seemed to know her so well. They didn't always have to speak to know what the other was thinking. She believed that they were so in sync with each other that they were like one. It seemed like the obvious decision to marry and become as one for life. But eventually the decisions he made on his own got bigger, and when she confronted him, his reply was always, "It's what you want, isn't it? I thought we were on the same page here."

The final straw had been the day she came home and found the "For Sale" sign in their yard. They had discussed selling the house and moving into a bigger one now that they could afford it, but to her knowledge there had been no decision made.

Once again, she confronted him. His reply was so predictable that she wondered why he didn't just record it so she only had to push the play button when she needed a response. "Honey, we've been talking about this for weeks. It's what you wanted, isn't it? I thought we were on the same page here."

Yes, they had discussed it. No, she wasn't sure it was what she wanted. They hadn't even started looking for a new place. Why did he always decide when their discussions were done and what they would do? That was when she had made her own decision. She decided to stay just where she was, and if he was so anxious to move, maybe he should, but a bachelor suite would probably be all the room he would need. That night he packed a bag and stayed in a hotel. Somehow, after he left, the house didn't seem so small after all.

Pat took a sip of her Singapore Sling, forcing her thoughts back to the present. Her only reply was, "Thank you."

The conversation started slowly and awkwardly, but Pat was pleasantly surprised that within minutes conversation became easier. The next two hours were two old acquaintances catching up. There was even some laughter. When it was time to leave, the two made plans for a family supper. Jack would join Pat, Nathan, and Chelsea at the house on Sunday.

Only one day earlier, this would have made Pat anxious as she anticipated problems. What if Jack or the kids saw this as the two of them getting back together? She knew she didn't want this, and over drinks, she realized that Jack didn't either. Between the two of them, they would convince Nathan and Chelsea that although their parents would remain friends and the four of them were still a family, each of their parents would continue to live separate lives.

Jack walked Pat to her car. "Thank you for meeting me. I wasn't sure you would. I may have screwed up and lost my wife, but I'm glad I haven't lost my friend."

"We both screwed up, Jack. I'll let the kids know you'll be joining us on Sunday."

Jack leaned over and placed a light kiss on Pat's cheek. "See you Sunday, around two o'clock."

By the time Pat got home, Kelly, the babysitter, had fed the kids, and they were ready for bed. Kelly was 16 and had been babysitting Nathan and Chelsea for the past two years. She was another reason Pat had hesitated about moving. Kelly was a wonderful babysitter, and the kids adored her. It was so convenient that she lived right next door.

"Oh, there's a message for you," Kelly remembered as she was walking out the door. "Someone named Gordon. I left his number by the phone."

Pat waited until finding out how Nathan and Chelsea's days were and tucked them in before returning the call. He answered on the second ring.

"Hello?"

"Gordon? It's Pat McDermott. I have a message that you called."

"Thanks for calling back. You must be a busy lady. You always seem to out when I call. Have you remembered who I am yet?"

"As a matter of fact, I have. I met you at Janine's party a few years ago."

"And have you had enough time to call Janine and check me out?"

Pat was silent. She had, in fact, phoned Janine the day after his last message, and she had received a raving review.

Gordon laughed. "I thought you might. So, tell me, did I pass?"

Pat felt her face suddenly become warm as she turned red from being caught. She was glad he was not there to see it. "So far," she replied.

"Is it possible for us to get together so you can make up your own mind?"

"I think that could be arranged."

"Great. How about tomorrow night? I could meet you after work for a drink, and maybe we could catch dinner after that."

"Sorry, I don't like to leave the kids with a babysitter two nights in a row."

"Okay, then. What about Friday? Instead of meeting after work, you could feed the kids . . . what are their names?"

"Nathan and Chelsea."

"You can feed Nathan and Chelsea supper and spend a little time with them, and then I'll pick you up at seven. The two of us will go to a restaurant where you can continue deciding about me while we eat. Do you like Italian food?"

"I love Italian food. Let me call my babysitter and find out if she is free for Friday. I'll call you back."

As Pat grabbed her briefcase to head into the Andrews' home, she continued to contemplate the degree to which both Nina's and her lives had changed from two weeks ago. She thought, it only goes to show if everything looks bleak and hopeless, hang on for dear life; good things may be just around the corner. And if everything is going your way, cherish every moment; the memories may be the only thing to give you strength and help you through the next stage in your life. This just might be the day everything turns around, whatever it is that is going on in your life.

Pat rang Nina's doorbell and put all thoughts of her own life to the side. As she stood on the step waiting, she began to concentrate on the business at hand.

When the door opened, a younger version of Mike Andrews stood in front of her. The resemblance was so great that there was no doubt in her mind that this was his son, Mark. Pat stood speechless until the young man extended his hand to greet her.

"Pat McDermott? How do you do? I'm Mark Andrews."

Pat reached for his hand. "I've heard a lot about you. I'm glad we finally get to meet. I'm just sorry it's under these circumstances."

"Thank you. Come in. My mother is in the kitchen."

As Pat entered the kitchen, she got her first glimpse of Nina since Mike's death. It had only been six months since their last meeting, but Pat barely recognized the woman standing by the kitchen counter.

When Nina turned to acknowledge her, Pat saw the dark circles under the other woman's eyes and noticed that any hint of a sparkle for life had left them. Pat had always been impressed with the way that Nina had presented herself. She never had a hair out of place, her makeup always perfect, and whatever she wore was put together elegantly.

There was no resemblance between that woman and the woman standing in front of her now wearing baggy sweatpants and an oversized T-shirt, something Pat didn't even think Nina owned. Nina's face was bare of any makeup, and the bags under her eyes showed the lack of sleep. She leaned against the counter looking as lifeless as her limp, unkempt hair.

If they had passed on the street, Pat would walked right by without even noticing her. Nina had aged at least 10 years since their last meeting. This was the walking robot that she had spoken to on the phone a couple days earlier.

With what could only be called a representation of a smile, Nina asked her company if she would like a coffee.

"Oh, please don't go to any trouble."

"It's no trouble at all. I live on coffee and cigarettes these days. Mark, why don't you and Pat sit down at the table, and I'll bring the coffee over."

Mark led Pat to the kitchen table, which had been cleared of all objects with the exception of a writing pad and pen.

As they sat Mark said, "I hope you don't mind, but I thought I'd take some notes."

"No problem. I have some material I can leave too. I imagine you will want a little time to go through everything and talk about it before making any decisions."

Nina brought over a tray that carried three cups of coffee, cream, and sugar. As she was carrying them, Pat heard two of the cups clink together. The tray was shaking from Nina's unsteadiness, and Pat had visions of wearing the contents. After putting the cups down, Nina turned and left the same way she entered. When she returned she was carrying a platter of cold meats, crackers, cheese, and fruit.

"You didn't need to go to all this trouble," Pat said, looking over the selection.

"Trust me," Nina replied, "it was no trouble. So many people are bringing food over these days. There is no way we will ever be able to eat it all—even if Mark were to stay a couple more weeks instead of only a couple more days."

As Nina sat next to Pat, she started to reach for a piece of fruit but then pulled her hand back. "I do appreciate the thought, but I'm not eating much these days. At least the kids don't have to starve."

An hour and a half after arriving, Pat left to return to the office. All things considered, she felt the meeting had gone well. They had reviewed the investments and life insurance, and then Nina gave Pat a copy of Mike's death certificate and signed the appropriate papers.

When Pat made her suggestions for Nina's financial future, she noticed that Mark listened carefully and made extensive notes. With Mark's background in banking and financial planning, he knew as much about the subject as the presenter did. Knowing this, Pat had asked Nina if she would be more comfortable having Mark take over the profile. It was Mark who answered.

"Out of the question. Not only do I think it is unethical, even though the practice has been approved, but I wouldn't feel comfortable either. I'm too close to the client. I would be nervous every time I gave any advice. If an investment I recommended lost money, I would feel like I should make up those losses out of my own pocket. I think for family peace, we'll leave everything in your capable hands. Besides, I know that Mom and Dad were happy with you, and from what I've seen, I can't see where I would suggest anything differently."

Pat left some literature on different matters and made sure all questions had been answered before leaving another business card on her way out. Nina and Mark wanted to consider everything discussed; one of them would get back to Pat before Mark left on Sunday.

As Pat organized her car for the trip back to the office, she took one last look at the Andrews' house and was grateful once again for the life she had, even as busy and stressful as it was. As she drove away, her thoughts once more went back to the evening before with Jack.

She knew that the arrangement they had agreed to would be better for everyone involved. She had physically felt a weight lift from her shoulders as they parted ways the night before.

Two blocks from the Andrews house, all thoughts of Nina and Jack were gone, and Pat was mentally going through her closet picking out an outfit for her date with Gordon on Friday night. Suddenly, she realized just how nervous she was.

It had been 12 years since her last first date, and she wasn't exactly sure what the proper protocol was anymore. She made a mental note to ask Nancy—assuming she would even know—and then merged onto the busy freeway, leaving all thoughts of clients, ex-husbands, kids and dates until later, while she concentrated on the heavy traffic.

Friday, August 24

PAT LOOKED AT ALL THE clothes lying on her bed. Each outfit had been tried on, scrutinized in the mirror, and discarded. When she finished her last appointment at 3:30, she had packed her briefcase with work to do at home over the weekend and left the office for the day.

Now at 6:45, she had spent time with Nathan and Chelsea, made sure they were fed and bathed, and then had taken a shower herself. Her makeup and hair were done, and now it was just a matter of finding the right outfit and accessories. Looking at her reflection in the mirror, Pat wasn't any more satisfied with this outfit than she had been with the last. Gordon was due in 15 minutes and Kelly in five. Maybe she could get Kelly's opinion. She could always change again before Gordon arrived if Kelly thought it was necessary.

Pat held her hand to her stomach, trying to calm the butterflies. This is ridiculous, she thought. I'm acting like a schoolgirl going out on her first date instead of a grown woman with two wonderful children and a successful business.

Just then the doorbell rang and she jumped. Hurrying to answer it, she silently prayed that it was Kelly and not Gordon arriving early. With the door and prayers both answered, Pat hurried her babysitter into the bedroom for a final verdict on the outfits. Kelly told her to keep on the outfit she was wearing. She then added the jacket from the second outfit Pat had tried on and picked out a simple pair of earrings and scarf for accessories.

Looking into the full-length mirror and reviewing the final creation, Pat was pleasantly surprised. She had never thought to match this jacket with this outfit before, but examining her reflection now, she discovered that it was an elegant look with a touch of sophistication.

When the doorbell rang a second time, Pat jumped again. Laughing, Kelly told her to just stay where she was for a minute; she would answer the door so that Pat could make an entrance. That way it would add a little mystery for him and give Pat time to calm down.

So, not much has changed, she thought as she watched Kelly head for the front door. Standing in her room, she listened as the two introduced themselves. After that, Nathan and Chelsea decided to play twenty questions with Gordon. "What's your name? Where are you taking our Mom? What do you do?"

Pat had talked to Nathan and Chelsea earlier about her date, and they had each seemed to accept it. She hoped it wasn't too soon for them—or her, for that matter. She had always been conscious of the fact that everything she said or did would affect them. Since her separation from their father, she had been even more conscious of this fact.

Pat wondered if every mother carried the same fear that she did. It was her fear that, as a mother, she would inevitably do something that would ruin the rest of her children's lives—and that it would be all her fault when they grew up to be dysfunctional adults. It had been her private battle from the time the doctor told her she was pregnant, and it had grown since she and their father had decided to part ways.

Then there was the guilt. Times like now, when she was going out with a man who was not their father, and when she let someone else read them a story and tuck them in at night. Pat had always been conscious of the fact that her every move, her every action was being watched by Nathan and Chelsea, and that whatever she said or did affected them.

She had taken on the sole responsibility of her children's actions and happiness. The emotional side of her couldn't stop, even though the logical side of her knew that by doing so, she was removing all responsibility from her children.

Pat had a small panic attack and was thinking of calling the date off when she heard giggles coming from the other room and realized that she was overreacting again. After all, it was just one date. It's not like she was about to introduce this man as their new father. They had a father, and he was coming over for dinner Sunday night. In the meantime, she had a date and he was waiting.

As Pat listened, she suddenly realized that not only did she allow a 16-year-old to decide what she would wear on her first date, but she had also allowed that same 16-year-old to decide how she would act. Stay here and wait a minute? Make an entrance? Wasn't she a little old for those games? Surely at her age the rules were a little different than at Kelly's age!

Besides, what was it that Kelly had murmured on her way out? Something like, "This is so cool. I never knew people your age got as nervous as the kids my age do before a date." Pat quickly turned out the light and hurried to the door.

Turning the corner to the hallway leading to the front entry, she caught her first glimpse of Gordon in three years. Wow, she thought, he's just as good looking as I remembered. Before anyone noticed her, she made her presence known.

"Gordon, sorry I kept you waiting. I see you've met the troops, though."

"Wow, you look great," he replied. Feeling her cheeks begin to warm from the compliment, she was grateful when he quickly added, "Nathan and Chelsea have just been getting my whole life story. I think if you had waited another minute, they would have asked for a blood sample."

"Wow," Nathan chirped, "that would be cool! Can we, Mom?"

"No," Pat replied simply. She grabbed her coat from the closet and spoke to Gordon. "I'm sorry. I've always taught them to be inquisitive, but sometimes they take it too far."

"Don't worry about it. Inquisitive is good."

Pat leaned over and gave each of her children a hug and a kiss. "Now, you listen to Kelly and be good." She stood up and Gordon opened the door for her. As they were leaving, she turned and told Kelly, "We shouldn't be late."

"Don't worry about us, we'll be fine. And be as late as you want. I'm saving my money to buy a car, so I could use the extra hours."

As the vehicle pulled out of the driveway, Pat said, "Again, I am so sorry for the twenty questions. It seems to be their favourite game; they even play it with me, so I know it can get a little tiring."

"Really, don't worry about it," he laughed. "I don't have any kids of my own, but I do have a niece and nephew that I see often. I know what kids are like. Actually, it's one of the things I haven't had in my life, and now I'm beginning to wonder if that was a mistake--not having kids, I mean.

"Don't get me wrong," he added quickly. "I've enjoyed my life and I feel very fortunate for what I have and what I've done, but sometimes I wonder what my life would be like now if I had settled down."

Pat looked over to him. *I think I like this man,* she thought. "Well, I believe that things happen for a reason and that we make decisions for a reason—even if we don't know why. If you had chosen to settle down, you wouldn't have the experiences you have had, so you wouldn't be the person you are today. Besides, it's not too late to settle down now, and you will probably appreciate it more now than you would have—say, 10 years ago."

"Wow, this is deeper than what I expected tonight. I thought that by the time I brought you home, we would have just covered the basic stuff like, 'What's your favourite colour?' and 'Where did you grow up?'"

"I'm sorry. You must really wonder what you've got yourself into tonight. First the 20 questions from the kids, then my philosophical views of life." Deciding to change the subject, she asked, "So tell me, where did you grow up?"

"There's nothing to be sorry about. I'm not ready to turn around and run, yet. I'm actually enjoying myself—and I grew up in Red Deer, although that's when it was only about half the size it is now. After graduation, I came to Calgary to go to university—which also, by the way, seems to have doubled in size. Except for the past couple of years when the company sent me down east to Toronto, I've lived here ever since."

"Did you like growing up in Red Deer?"

Conversation for the remainder of the evening was a lot lighter than it had started out, and Pat found herself enjoying his company very much. By the time he walked her to her door, she knew she wanted to see him again.

"Would you like to come in for coffee?"

"No, I better not, but if it's okay with you, I'd like to give you a call sometime again."

Pat felt her stomach do a little flip and silently reprimanded herself. Would you stop being such a schoolgirl and get a grip? she scolded herself. He only said he wants to call you again.

"That would be great," was all she said.

"Fine. I'll give you a call sometime soon. Thank you for this evening. I really enjoyed myself," he said, and then he turned and left.

Pat stood on her front step and watched as he walked to his car. She had been hoping that he would come in for coffee. She had also been looking forward to a goodnight kiss. Maybe he didn't really enjoy himself, and she just got the brush-off. If that were true, she wondered, why would he make a point of saying he had enjoyed himself and wanted to see her again?

As he opened his car door, she opened the door of her home and stepped through. Maybe he just felt it was the polite thing to do. Pat shut the door behind her and silently told herself to give it a rest. It was not like the end of the world would come if he didn't call.

Kelly must have been waiting for her, because before Pat could get her coat off, her babysitter was right beside her playing the same 20 question game that the kids had played with Gordon earlier.

"So, what was he like? Did you have a good time? Do you think he'll call again?"

"He was very nice, I had a good time, and I don't know if he'll call again or not. Now, the more important questions are, How were the kids? Did they give you any trouble? Were there any problems?"

"The kids were great, they were no trouble, there weren't any problems, and I'll mind my own business."

After putting on her coat, Kelly added as she was leaving, "If you do like him, I hope he does call you again. He seemed really nice."

"Thank you, Kelly—for everything. Goodnight."

"Goodnight."

~ ~ ~ ~ ~ ~ ~ ~ ~ ~ ~ ~ ~ ~ ~ ~ ~ ~

As Pat was leaving for her date with Gordon, Nina was reaching into the liquor cabinet for a bottle of red wine. It was going to be another long evening of filling in the minutes. She had never realized before just how many minutes there were in an evening, or just how long a minute could last.

The kids had gone back to their own lives and busy routines. Mark had planned on staying until the end of the weekend, but something had come up at work, and they had asked him to come back early.

Nina could remember him explaining the sudden need to return, but she found that she was not retaining much information these days. No matter how hard she tried, she couldn't remember what it was that had called him back.

She did remember that he had offered to come back for the weekend, but this was already his second trip home since Mike had been brought to the hospital, so Nina had convinced him that she would be fine.

Georgia, her coworker from the office and friend, and Mark had both phoned earlier to see how she was doing on her own. That filled in half an hour. The rest of the evening was hers to fill, and hers alone.

Maybe it was time to go back to work, she reasoned. She worked part-time in a small office, and her boss had told her to take as much time as she needed; the job would be waiting for her when she was ready to return. She wasn't sure she was ready, but the days were long and the nights were longer. She needed to do something to fill her time. She was fortunate that Mike had been financially responsible, and because of that, she was allowed the privilege of choice. She just wasn't sure she was capable of choice right now.

Maybe if someone told her she had to go back to work, she would go back into the office and she would handle it.

But she was so afraid of breaking down; the office was no place for that.

What if people started telling her how sorry they were, and then she cried in front of them—right there in the office? What if she couldn't do the work she was paid to do, because she couldn't concentrate? And how could she walk into the empty house each night knowing that she couldn't talk to Mike about her day?

Nina poured some of the red wine into a glass, put the bottle back, and took a sip. If she didn't know what to do with a day or an evening, what was she going to do with the rest of her life?

It had been 12 days since she found him in the backyard. Did anyone else know exactly how many days and nights had passed, or were they already "arounding"? "It was *around* two weeks ago, wasn't it?" was probably closer to the way they remembered it.

It seemed inconceivable to Nina that life was already going on as normal for everyone else. Their lives had probably returned to the way it had been *around* two weeks ago. Except for Mark and Jan. She knew they missed their father and worried about their mother, which is why she tried to sound as positive as she could whenever they called.

Tonight had been hard, though—harder than usual. Nina had made it through the day, doing little chores like washing the kitchen floor, picking up groceries for the next day, anything to make time pass. She had even bought frozen lasagna and a bag of salad so that she could have an actual meal.

While the lasagna heated in the oven, she placed some of the salad in a bowl, covered it with salad dressing, and then sat at her place at the table to eat it. As she put the fork to mouth, she looked over at the empty chair across from her and realized how alone she was. Tears welled in her eyes, and she put the fork down. She couldn't do this.

She picked the bowl up, returned to the kitchen, and leaned against the counter to eat it there, but she had trouble forcing it down her throat. After only one bite, she threw the salad in the garbage and got her plate out for the lasagna. Maybe hot food would go down better. Holding the plate in hand, she was about to pitch her fork into the food when a car horn honked outside. Startled, she jumped, and the plate she was holding dropped to the floor.

Looking at the mess of spilled lasagna on the floor she had just washed a few hours before, the tears welled up once again. She knelt down to pick up the lasagna and put it back on her plate before throwing it out. Soon the tears were streaming down her face.

Feeling defeated, she dropped the plate again and collapsed into a ball on the floor. She never noticed the lasagna on her hands as she covered her face and sobbed. Suddenly, she heard screaming and quickly realized it was her.

This was the first time since her nightmare began 12 days ago that she allowed herself the luxury of not worrying about upsetting anyone around her, and she just let the pain out. Never in her life could she remember such heart-wrenching pain. She was angry at the world and everyone in it. They may not have been responsible, but they still had their lives; the same lives they had yesterday and the day before that, and that angered her.

Sitting on the kitchen floor beside her spilled lasagna, Nina was surprised that she was also angry at Mike for leaving. "Why?" she called out between sobs. "Why did you go, Mike? Why did you leave me?"

Reasoning that Mike hadn't left her but that he had been taken, her anger turned towards heaven for the injustice that had been done. Immediately she knew in her mind who it was that was responsible for everything that had happened, and for everything she had lost. She turned her focus to where she knew the blame lay.

"Why did You take him, God? His whole life Mike worked hard, helped others, and always did the right thing. Why would You take him now, when he was about to reap the joy of his labour?"

Maybe if she reasoned with Him calmly, He would realize His mistake and correct it.

"I think You made a mistake, God, but You can fix it because You *are* God. You can undo what has been done."

Not getting an answer as quickly as she wanted, her anger returned.

"I don't understand! Make me understand!" she shouted as she shook her fist to heaven.

Twenty minutes later, Nina wiped her tears and her runny nose on the sleeve of her sweatshirt, still asking the questions, but it was in a hoarse whisper now. "Please, someone, help me. Help me understand why this has happened."

She cried until she cried herself out. Weak and drained, she slowly picked herself up and made her way to the bathroom. There she blew her nose and washed her face. Feeling a little more composed, she made her way back to the kitchen to finish the task at hand.

It wasn't until the mess was cleaned up and the container holding the remainder of the lasagna was covered and put away that she reached for the glass of red wine that she had poured earlier. While she was sitting on the deck finally drinking the wine and smoking a cigarette, the phone rang. The noise made her jump again, but this time nothing spilled. She debated about answering it until she saw the number. It was Jan. She knew that if she didn't answer, Jan would probably worry.

"Hello?"

"Mom, are you okay? Your voice sounds hoarse. Have you been crying?"

"I think I might be getting a cold. When we hang up, I think I'll soak in the tub and get to bed early, see if I can beat it."

Jan wasn't completely convinced, but she didn't push any further. "How was your day?"

"Pretty good. I did some running around, cleaned the house. Nothing too exciting. How about you, Dear? How was your day?"

Jan hesitated. "It was fine. Mom, are you sure you're okay?"

"I'm fine. In fact, I made myself some salad and lasagna tonight. I just finished cleaning up and I'm sitting on the deck enjoying a glass of wine."

"Got any plans for the weekend, Mom?"

"Well, we'll see how this cold is. I thought maybe I'd get a little yard work done. Nothing special."

Nina recalled an earlier conversation when Jan had talked about her plans to play a game of golf with a girlfriend, and then she had a date later that evening. "You've got a full weekend, don't you?"

Nina noticed the pause before Jan answered.

"Actually the reason I'm calling, Mom, is because it turns out I don't have any plans this weekend, so I thought I'd come down. I'll be there before noon and we can go out for lunch. How does that sound?"

"Jan, I thought you were looking forward to this weekend. Please don't cancel your plans for me. I'll be fine."

"Mom, I want to come down."

Nina heard the quiver in her voice. Not knowing if Jan was coming down for her mother's sake, or because she needed too, Nina accepted. Maybe they needed each other.

Wednesday, September 12

THE SOUNDS OF THE OUTSIDE world filtered through Nina's bedroom window as she lay on her bed staring at the ceiling. She hadn't bothered to close the curtains the night before, and now the sun came through, beating down on her. The blankets had been kicked to one side as she tried to fend off the heat. She knew she should have been up an hour ago, but what was the point? What would make today different from any other day? Would anyone else remember that the hell she was living in had started one month ago today?

Suddenly she remembered that that morning had started much the same as today, with her lying in bed and not wanting to get up. She abruptly jumped out of bed. The memory of that morning brought on a fear, or more of an anxiety, really. Somehow she just knew that if she stayed in bed any longer, something terrible would happen. She wasn't sure what would happen, or why staying in bed would cause terrible things to happen, but for some unexplainable reason, she knew she had to get up, and she had to get up now.

Passing through the family room to the kitchen, she didn't notice the empty wineglass and the dirty ashtray on the coffee table. Until a month ago, the wineglass would have been washed, the ashes from the ashtray would have been flushed, and both would have been put away before going to bed the night before. Nina had always made sure that the house was a clean, tidy home. It was a home where many visited. All guests, whether they were invited or not, were made to feel welcome.

In the kitchen, Nina barely noticed the dirty dishes by the sink. The only time she picked up now was when she knew someone was coming over. Nothing had been picked up in three days.

Leaning against the counter, Nina looked around the kitchen for something she could just pop into her mouth and call breakfast. She knew she had to eat, but most of the time she still had no appetite, and it was a chore she had to force herself to perform. During the past month, she had lost 15 pounds.

As she glanced over the counter top for something to eat, she noticed the phone beside the newspapers that were piling up unread. Slowly, she picked up the receiver and listened for a dial tone. The phone calls and visits from friends and neighbours were getting fewer and farther between.

I guess after a month I'm supposed to be ready to put the past behind me and move on with a life without Mike. Are they right? she wondered as she made her way back to the bedroom, all thoughts of breakfast forgotten. Is there a proper length of time to grieve that I have exceeded? she asked herself while pulling on an old pair of blue jeans. What is the proper time? Let me see, if it's been a month, and I've exceeded the proper mourning time, maybe I'm only supposed to mourn one day for every year we were together. Is that all I'm allowed for my life with Mike? Am I really supposed to be ready to get on with my life now?

Then she thought angrily, What the hell do they know about it? All these people, who were so willing to give me food and advice, sympathy and companionship in the beginning, have now decided that I should move on with my life, but they have no idea what I'm going through. How could they? None of them have been through it.

Nina realized that the numbness she felt a month ago was gone and had slowly been replaced with emotions—emotions which she didn't want to feel. She preferred the numbness, because the emotions of self-pity, anger, sorrow, bitterness, and self-doubt were much harder to handle. At least with numbness, there was no pain.

She recognized that she had felt every emotion at some time in her life, but never, ever had they been so intense. Now the emotions overpowered her and controlled her. At times she was afraid, and on occasion the fear grew so relentless that it would immobilize her. But she never knew exactly what it was that she was afraid of, and that alone scared her.

At times like this, when she became so angry at the world, including everybody and nobody in particular, she had to scream out. The sensation was so compelling that it brought on a throbbing in her head that was often followed by a sharp pain. The severity of the pain caused her to hold her head and wonder if she was going crazy. She would crumble to the floor and pray that the pain in her head was being caused by a stroke, just like the one that Mike had. If only it were so, she thought. If I could just die of a stroke like Mike, we could be together once again.

Nina returned to the bedroom, glanced at the unmade bed, thought of making it, and then turned and left the room. Feeling claustrophobic but having no desire to leave the house, Nina stood by the patio doors and looked out at the backyard. Summer was ending, and the cool nights had turned the leaves to yellows and oranges before the branches released them and dropped them to the ground. The yard was now covered with leaves.

The yard had always been Mike's domain. He had spent hours outside mowing, trimming, and raking. It was where he'd found peace, and he'd had little patience for anyone who had an unkempt yard, just as Nina had always had little patience for a dirty house. She knew he would be disgusted with the way the yard looked now.

Suddenly Nina was disgusted with herself for letting the yard get to the state it was in. She pulled on a sweater, went to the garage, found the rake, and began raking the leaves. She had been at the task for half an hour when she heard the rustle of leaves behind her. Straightening her back, she turned to see Carrie from next door.

"Good morning, Nina."

"Hello," Nina replied. Nina didn't realize it, but until a month ago she had always greeted everyone with a chipper "Good morning!" Subconsciously, she would not allow herself to greet anyone with anything that started with "Good." Although Nina never noticed, this fact never went unnoticed by Carrie.

"I was going to call you later," Carrie said. "Scott and I have been talking about having you over for supper, and when I saw you in the yard, I decided to just come over and ask you in person. I'm not working today, so why don't you come over about six tonight? It will just be the three of us."

Nina leaned on the rake. For reasons beyond her understanding, she was fighting back the tears because of this simple invitation to supper. Maybe it was because the calls and visits from concerned friends were coming further apart, and the gesture meant more to her than even Nina realized. Or maybe it was because everything seemed to make her cry these days.

Nina felt the turmoil inside. As much as she craved company and someone to talk to, she was afraid of losing control of her emotions in front of people, even friends as wonderful as Scott and Carrie. She also knew that the thought of another evening home alone was unbearable.

"Is there anything I can bring?" Nina finally asked, her decision made.

"No. It's just the three of us for a simple supper, nothing fancy. Well, I was just on my way to the store to pick up a few things, so I'd better get going. It seems like every time I have a day off, I work just as hard as the days I actually go in to the office, so in the end, it's not really a day off anyway." She chuckled. "Oh, for a day of rest." Carrie was still shaking her head and laughing softly when she turned to leave. She had no sooner turned away when she turned back again. "Did you need anything picked up while I'm out?"

Nina realized that Carrie was babbling now, perhaps to avoid any more awkward pauses.

"No, thanks."

"Okay, well, we'll see you about six then."

Nina spent the next few hours raking and bagging the leaves. When the job was done, she decided to go inside and put on a pot of coffee. Hopefully, the hot liquid would warm her. The cool fall days always brought a chill, and Nina had noticed that over the past few years, she felt it right to her bones. A part of aging, she had reasoned.

As she reached for the doorknob to go inside, her heart rate began to escalate. Within seconds her heart was pounding, and she swore she could feel her heart hit her ribcage with every beat. Her hand froze in mid-air, and her feet froze to the ground where she stood. She could not bring herself to go in. Suddenly, the same anxiety that had forced her to leave her bed so abruptly only a few hours earlier washed over her once again.

This is ridiculous, she thought. Taking a deep breath, she forced herself to turn the doorknob and then slowly opened the door. She felt her heart racing a mile a minute. She wondered if she was about pass out. Just as she was about to step in, she quickly closed the door.

What is wrong with me? Why can't I enter my own home? She didn't understand her emotions these days and she went back to the steps of the deck, sat down, and lit a cigarette.

I think I'm losing my mind, she thought. What am I supposed to do? What do I do next? Please help me, she silently prayed. I just don't know what to do.

When she slowly got up from the steps, she had every intention of trying the door one more time. Without realizing where she was going, however, she found herself standing at the spot where she had discovered Mike laying on the ground. Help me, Mike, she silently pleaded. My whole life was planned around you, but you left. You left me all alone, and I don't know what to do! Tears ran down her cheeks.

With a feeling of absolutely no control over her body, Nina sat on the ground next to where Mike had laid. If anyone had been watching from a distance, it would have looked like a scene from the movie screen being played back in slow motion. With her back against the house, she brought her knees up to her chin and sat there staring at the spot she had found him.

"You son of a bitch," she whispered. "You left me. Now there is no plan. There is no plan without you, and nobody understands that." Smothering a sob with her hands so that no one walking by could hear, she slowly began to rock back and forth and buried her face. "I don't understand why you left. If there is a God, he isn't perfect, because this time He made a mistake. He made the mistake, but I have to live with it."

After a few minutes, Nina wiped her tears, stood, and slowly found her way back to the same door she had tried to enter earlier. With a shaky hand and through blurred vision, she tentatively entered.

She wandered the house aimlessly, still not seeing the dirty dishes in the sink, the papers piled up on the counter, or the dirty wineglass and ashtray sitting on the dusty coffee table, until finally she was standing in the middle of her bedroom where the bed was still unmade. She laid herself on the bed, snuggled up to a pillow, and covered herself. Within minutes, she was asleep on a pillow damp with tears.

It was the shrill sound of ringing that woke Nina two hours later. Feeling for the phone, she picked up the receiver on the third ring.

"Hello?"

"Nina?"

"Yes."

"This is Grant from the office. I'm sorry, did I wake you?"

"No...well, yes, but that's okay. If I sleep too long I won't sleep tonight."

"Maybe I should call back later."

"No, no, this is fine. I just sat up and I'm awake now. Did you need something, Grant?"

"Well, kind of, but first, how are you doing?"

"I'm fine," Nina lied. No sense in telling him the truth, she thought. It would just make him uncomfortable and sorry he had asked. She'd already made the mistake of answering that question truthfully once before. When the other person's response to her reply was to become silent and quietly exit, she vowed never to make that mistake again. Her standard reply now was always, "I'm fine."

"Nina, I have a favour to ask you. Is it possible to come into the office so we can talk?"

"Today?"

"If you like, but if that's inconvenient, tomorrow is fine."

Nina glanced at the clock radio on her nightstand: 2:30. Half of the afternoon was already gone.

"Maybe tomorrow would be better. I'll be in the office at ten o'clock. Is that all right with you?"

"Great. Thanks, Nina. I'll see you tomorrow."

Nina hung up the phone. The sleep had helped. She felt better than she had two hours earlier and was now grateful that she had accepted Carrie's invitation. As she washed her face, she realized that she was actually looking forward to going out this evening.

This time, she made the bed before leaving the room. On her way through the family room, she picked up the wineglass and ashtray, and when she got to the kitchen, she filled the sink with water and washed the dishes.

It's amazing what a little sleep and a phone call from the outside world can do, she thought. Nina tidied the house, showered, and picked up a bouquet of flowers for her hosts. At six o'clock sharp, she was standing on the front steps of the house next to hers and ringing the doorbell. As she waited for the door to open, she was surprised and amazed at the realization of how much someone else's company meant to her.

When Scott answered the door, she greeted him with a smile and walked in as he held it open for her. Carrie came out from the kitchen to greet her and Nina handed her the bouquet. "Here, these are for you," she said. She handed a bottle of Grand Marnier to Scott and said, "I thought we could have this with our coffee after supper."

Thursday, September 13

PAT SIPPED ON HER COFFEE at her desk as she read one of the many financial magazines to which she subscribed. She had discovered a few years earlier that after getting herself, Chelsea, and Nathan ready and out the door each morning, she handled the stresses of the office a lot better when she was able to fit 15 minutes of "Pat time" in before getting on with the day.

Nancy knew the routine and took phone messages, allowing no one through. The rule was not to interrupt Pat during this time unless it was an emergency, such as the school phoning about one of the children, or someone dying. Everything else was to be put on hold until nine o'clock.

Pat was just about to grab her coffee mug when Nancy's voice came over the intercom.

"Good morning, boss. It's the new love of your life on line one. Do you want me to tell him it's 'Pat time' and take a message?"

Pat felt the butterflies begin to flutter in her stomach. They were the same butterflies that had appeared the evening she and Gordon went out on their first date. They reappeared every time she heard his voice or knew that she was about to.

After their first date, Pat wondered more than once if it would be proper for her to phone him, but in the end, he called first. It was the longest four days Pat could recall as she had waited for the phone to ring. Unlike the first date, when he brought her home, after the second date, he came in for coffee. When he left two hours later, he gave her a goodnight kiss that left her knees weak.

"Nancy, I have asked you not to call him that. We've only been seeing each other a few weeks, and I'm not about to get into anything serious yet. My divorce isn't even final, for heaven's sake." Then Pat realized that she was getting too defensive over a teasing remark, and she simply said, "Oh, never mind," and picked up line one.

"Hello?"

"Good morning, Gorgeous. You know, you just might get me fired."

"Me? I've never even seen your office."

"I know, but it's because of you that I can't get any work done. I keep thinking about the last time I saw you and wonder when I can see you again. The next thing you know, I'm fighting to beat a deadline."

"Well, what you need, Mr. Atkins, is better concentration."

"Oh, there's nothing wrong with my concentration. It's the subject that I choose to concentrate on. How about seeing me tonight?"

"I can't. It's meet the teachers night for Chelsea and Nathan."

"What time is that?"

"Seven thirty."

"Then meet me for a drink after work. Just one, then you can go meet the teachers, and I can go home and dream about you."

"Yeah, that would leave a good impression. Meet the teacher with alcohol on my breath."

"Okay, coffee."

Pat was tempted, but instead she replied, "Gordon, I'm really sorry. You knew when we started dating that Nathan and Chelsea were my priorities. After work, I am going to go home, feed them supper, and find out how their days were."

"You are absolutely right. They are, and should be, your first consideration. Do you want me to come over and stay with them while you go to your meetings?"

"No thanks. I've already booked Kelly. Don't forget, she wants the money for that car she's dreaming about."

"Okay, well, just hearing your voice will have to be enough so I can concentrate and get some work done."

There was just a bit of a pause on the phone, then, "Pat?"

"Yes?"

"Am I moving too fast?"

"I don't know," she answered honestly. "I really want to take it slow, for my sake as well as the kids', but I really do enjoy our time together." She let out a small sigh. "I wasn't expecting you, Gordon. Let's take it one day at a time and just see what happens."

"I've already made up my mind, Pat, so you pick the speed this relationship goes. I'll just have to adjust to that speed."

Pat hung up the phone and picked up her coffee, which had gone cold. He'd already made up his mind? That scared her just a little—but it pleased her too. She had wanted more time before being in another serious relationship. Time for the kids to adjust. Time for her to adjust. Time to figure out what it was that she had done wrong that had contributed to the breakup of her marriage.

Pat stared at the phone. She knew it would be tough, but she had to keep things from progressing too fast. She also knew that she wanted to see where it would end up.

"Pat." Nancy's voice came over the intercom for the second time that morning. "Mrs. Laden is on the phone. Do you want to speak with her, or should I take a message?"

"Thanks, Nancy, I'll take it."

～～～～～～～～～～～～～～～～～～

Nina waited for the elevator in the office building she had worked in for the past six years. She was a little apprehensive about her meeting with Grant. With the exception of Georgia, her long-time friend and coworker who had been in contact with her at least once a week since Mike's funeral, Nina had not had any contact with anyone from the office, until Grant's phone call yesterday.

Maybe this was a mistake, she thought. Just as she was debating with the idea of turning around and going home, the elevator doors opened. She was grateful to see that it was empty, tentatively stepped in, and pushed the button for the fifth floor. The elevator rose without stopping to pick up any other passenger. By the time the elevator doors opened again, she was shaking and wondered if she was going to be sick. Needing time to calm her nerves, she turned right when she stepped out of the elevator, towards the public washroom, instead of left, which was the direction of the office. Inside one of the stalls, Nina leaned against the door, breathing deeply. She could feel her heart pounding in her chest.

Silently, she talked herself out of turning around and heading home and composed herself as best she could. Her heart rate slowed, and she began to feel more in control. She took one last deep breath and opened the stall door. She turned the water faucet on and let the cold water run over her wrists, a trick she had read about several years ago to calm nerves. Feeling somewhat better, she dried her wrists and headed out the door and down the hall for the office before she had time to think about it.

By the time she was standing outside the office door, her heart was starting to pound again. Determined not to be defeated by her fear, she stopped, hesitated just a moment to summon up as much willpower as she could, and turned the handle.

At the sound of the door opening, Toni, the receptionist, looked up from her desk. Nina had tried to time her arrival during Toni's morning break but had obviously failed.

"Nina!" she exclaimed as she got up from her desk and walked around it to give Nina a big hug. Nina stood perfectly still, allowing Toni her act of affection but refusing to hug her back.

"How *are* you?" she asked in the condescending tone that Nina had learned to hate over the years. Toni sounded anything but sincere to Nina. Toni may not always have been the first to be concerned, but she was definitely the most dramatic. Nina felt her eyes begin to well with tears, but with sheer determination she was able to keep them from escaping.

"Oh, I just can't tell you how often I've thought of you, you poor thing," Toni gushed. "Every day I think of you. I want to phone or come over, but I *know* you just want to be left alone. If you need for anything, I'm sure you know that all you have to do is call me, and I'll do anything I can. You've known me long enough to know that I always put others ahead of myself. A downfall on my part, I suppose, but one that hopefully you will benefit from.

"In fact," she rambled on, "when I heard you were coming in today, I told my husband that if there was anything you needed, well, I would just have to drop everything I was doing and go to you. He will just have to understand that I can't be there for him all the time. Sometimes other people may need me too."

Nina no longer felt the impulse to cry, and instead she fought the urge to strike Toni. Maybe she could get off for mental instability. She was sure that everyone in the office would testify that they had each had an impulse to hit Toni at least once, and with all that "poor Nina" had been through ...well, who could expect her to have complete control over her emotions. Surely it was bound to happen.

Nina had convinced herself that she could get away with it when the office door leading to Georgia's office opened.

"I thought that was you. Why don't you come into my office? There's something I need to ask you."

Once they were in Georgia's office, behind closed doors, Nina collapsed into a chair in the corner by a small round table.

"Thanks. What took you so long?"

"I was on the phone and hadn't realized you were here. As soon as I heard Toni gushing all over you, I got rid of the person on the other end as quickly as I could and came out."

"I'm sure she means well," Nina said half-heartedly.

"In a pig's eye. She just has a way of centering all the attention around her somehow. It doesn't matter who is going through what, or how bad the situation is; somehow she becomes the main attraction."

Both girls giggled, but Nina's demeanor sobered once again. "If there's one thing I've learned since Mike died, Georgia, it's that nobody knows what to say to a grieving widow. Most people either want to give advice about something they know nothing about, or they want to avoid the subject altogether."

Georgia looked at her friend with compassion. "I know it's been tough for you. You're looking more rested than the last time I saw you. I'm really glad you agreed to come in today."

"What does Grant want to discuss, do you know?"

"I do. He ran it by me before he phoned you, but I told him I wouldn't talk to you about it until he discussed it with you first. Why don't we see if he's available now, and then we can go downstairs for a coffee and talk about it after you two have talked?"

"Okay." Nina felt the apprehension from before begin to return.

On the way to Grant's office, Nina noticed a man sitting behind the desk as they passed the door of her office. Not saying a word, she looked over to Georgia and then back to the office. Georgia followed Nina's line of vision and said, "Come in and meet Matt," turning from their original course and into the office that Nina had often referred to as her home away from home. Nina followed and Matt stood as the two entered.

"Matt," Georgia said, "this is Nina. This is her office that you are temporarily using. Nina, this is Matt. Grant hired him until you're ready to come back."

Matt stuck out his hand to shake Nina's. "How do you do? I promise that as soon as you say the word, I'm out of here."

Nina looked around for her personal belongings. Any sign that she had once occupied this office were gone, including the picture of her, Mike, Mark, and Jan. She was about to ask, but Georgia answered before she got the chance.

"I put your things in a box that is in my office. There was no need to drop them off at your place, because as soon as you are ready to come back, we just have to bring them back again."

"It's nice to meet you," Nina said to Matt, although, she wasn't sure how much truth there was in her statement. What was this man doing in her office? Were they making plans to replace her? It didn't sound like it; Georgia had said it was only until she returned.

Nina hadn't even thought of coming back to work, so she was surprised at how much it bothered her to find someone else using her office. She had a lot of questions for Georgia later. After the quick introduction, the two continued their way to Grant's office.

Grant was grateful for Georgia's presence. He was conscious of the fact that, except for his phone call yesterday, he had not even attempted to contact Nina since the funeral. Although he had thought of her often and had even picked up the phone to call a few times, he always hung up before dialing the last number. He had no idea what to say or what he would do if she started to cry. He had thought of having his wife, Janet, call, but he knew that if anyone called, it should be him.

So instead he thought of her often and said nothing of the guilt he felt. When there was office business to be discussed, he'd always had Georgia call—until yesterday, when she had surprised him by refusing.

He was the manager of the office, and no one refused a direct command from him; he simply wouldn't tolcrate it. During the eight years they had worked together, Georgia had never backed down from giving her opinion on the subject at hand, even if it meant disagreeing with Grant, but she knew that Grant had the final say and, agree or not, in the end Georgia followed the direction of her manager.

Grant had called Georgia into his office and gone over his plan for Nina with her. After hearing what he was suggesting, she had readily approved, as he hoped she would. It wasn't until he instructed her to phone Nina to make the arrangements, and she had flatly refused, that he found himself at a loss for words. Never had anyone under his supervision refused him before. He simply stood there, mouth open, as Georgia turned and walked away.

She stopped at the doorway and turned back. "Sometimes, Grant, you just have to do these things yourself, even if you are uncomfortable with them." With that, she was gone.

As he looked at Nina now, he didn't recognize the woman in front of him. She had lost so much weight that her clothes hung loosely. She looked old and tired.

Her eyes had always sparkled and had been full of mischief. Her eyes had smiled before her lips did; now they were dull and absent of emotion, with dark circles under them. She looked like she needed a week straight of sleep.

It was obvious that she didn't want to be there. Grant felt the urge to walk over, put his arms around her, and protect her from any more hurt. Instead, he chose to walk over and put an arm gently around her shoulders, for fear of breaking her both emotionally and physically, and he guided her to the chair across from his desk.

"Well, I'll leave you two alone," Georgia stated.

Before she could close the door, Grant asked, "Are you sure you don't want to stay?"

Georgia seemed to recognize the fear in his voice and knew that he would prefer her to stay, but she said, "No, I think it's better that I go and leave you two alone. Nina, don't forget we're going for coffee when you're done here," and with that she closed the door.

Grant ran his hand through his hair; something he tended to do when he was nervous. "Nina," he began, "We've got a project that we need done, and I think it would be perfect for you. You were—are," he corrected himself, "the most knowledgeable person in the office when it comes to our computer program, and you know our business. We purchased a new program that will make our record keeping a lot easier once it's up and running. The only problem with a new program is that, initially, we have to input a lot of the information ourselves. We can't download a lot of it.

"What I am proposing is that we contract you for that job. You can come in here and work whatever hours you want, or you can do it from home; it's totally up to you. Our fiscal year-end, as you know, is November 30, and we would like to begin the new fiscal year with this program. The only commitment I need from you is that it will be done by then."

Grant paused then, giving her time to let the proposal sink in. She hadn't said a word since she sat down. He watched for her reaction, but she just sat there, staring at an object on his desk with a distant look on her face. Had she even heard him? It wasn't long before the silence was more than he could endure.

"If you want to think about it, I understand, but I do think it would be good for both of us. I know you're going through a tough time right now, Nina, but maybe this will help give you something else to think about."

Her eyes left the object on his desk, and she looked up at him. He didn't need to see the expression on her face to realize what a stupid thing he had just said. When he was uncomfortable, he always stuck his foot in his mouth. It was the fear of doing something stupid like this that had stopped him from completing his phone calls to her.

"I'm so sorry, Nina, please forgive me. For me to even imply that our new program will replace Mike or take your mind off what's happening in your life was so insensitive of me." Was he just digging himself deeper?

"No, it wasn't insensitive, Grant. Just naïve," she said, and with that she stood up. "I have to think about it. Would it be all right if I got back to you?"

"Of course," he replied as he walked her to the door. As he opened the door for her, he placed his hand on her shoulder, and she looked up.

"I truly am sorry about Mike, Nina." He had only compassion and concern in his voice. "I had as high a regard for him as I do you, and I'm sorry I haven't been in touch. Whether you want to do this or not, is entirely up to you, but I promise you that either way, Janet and I will be in touch."

She simply nodded to acknowledge what he said, turned, and left.

Before Nina could stop it, one single tear rolled down her cheek. Ignoring Toni's calls to her and without stopping at Georgia's office as she had promised, she left the office and headed straight for her car. Afraid that the elevator might take too long and that Georgia would come looking for her, she ran down the stairs.

Pulling into her driveway 20 minutes later, she realized that all memory of the drive home was gone. She didn't know how she managed to make it through the traffic, but she was grateful that she hadn't caused an accident or killed anyone. Once inside the garage, Nina put the car into PARK and reached to turn off the ignition.

Slowly she pulled her hand away from the ignition and sat back. *If I just leave the car running and close the garage door, my pain could be over in a very short time.* The thought gave her comfort. At that, she leaned back, placing her head on the headrest and closed her eyes. *It won't be long, and I'll be with Mike again.*

It was several hours later that she called Georgia to apologize for running out on her. When she finally entered the house, after what she considered chickening out from any attempt of suicide, there was a message from Georgia. Nina knew she should phone back right away, but she needed time to see if she could figure things out. She had no idea what was happening to her or how to control it anymore.

When she did call, Nina explained the emotions that she was feeling when she left the office and that she couldn't remember her drive home, but she made a point of not mentioning her thoughts of suicide. Georgia accepted the apology and offered to come over right away, but Nina put her off. "No, I'm fine now. Don't worry about me," she had said.

"Nina," Georgia added just before they hung up, "about Matt. He came in looking for a job a week ago, and we needed someone, but it was explained to him that it was temporary, and the minute you say you're ready to come back, the position and office are yours again."

"I'm not really being fair to you, Grant, or anyone else in the office, am I?" she asked.

"Don't worry about it. With Matt here now, things are a lot easier, and he's perfectly fine with the situation being temporary. In fact, he said that suited him better. He only wants it temporarily and hopes you come back soon."

"I'll try and get things together, I promise. I'll talk to you later, okay?" With that she hung up, plopped herself down on the chesterfield and stared at a blank television for the next hour. Nina wasn't sure where her mind was during that hour. She knew she hadn't slept, but she couldn't remember a single thought she'd had during that time. Maybe she really was going crazy.

After supper, she spoke with Mark first and then Jan, before she considered accepting Grant's offer. Both Mark and Jan thought it would be good for her.

Later, over her daily glass of wine, she went over the events of the day. Everyone she had spoken with was encouraging her to take on this project. She had to admit that it felt good sitting in Georgia's office giggling. It was the first time she could remember feeling even a little bit normal in a long time.

Besides, she knew that if it didn't work out, Grant would understand. Plus, he had said that she would be able to do most of it from home if she wanted. She made up her mind then to phone Grant and accept on a "day by day" basis.

Saturday, September 15

PAT WAS LYING ON A lounge chair on the deck of a cruise ship, with the heat of the sun warming her and a large-brimmed straw hat keeping her face shaded. The cool ocean breeze swept over her, keeping her from getting too warm. She held the trashy romance novel she was reading in one hand and the special drink of the day in her other. Taking a sip from the glass, she wondered which ingredient it was that made the liquid so blue before quickly deciding she really didn't care. All she knew was that life couldn't get any better than this.

Suddenly the ship began to sway. The strength of the swaying increased, forcing her to sit up abruptly; the unexpected motion caused her to spill her drink. The waves of the ocean grew stronger. Both objects dropped from her hands. Nathan was yelling for her. He needed her! Where was he? Were they in danger? Maybe she should run for the life jackets.

"Mom! Wake up. Mom! Is it time to get up yet?"

Pat woke immediately, realizing that the rocking ship was nothing more than the movement of her bed from Nathan jumping on it. Still groggy and not wanting to leave her dream, she opened one eye to look at the clock radio on her nightstand and then let out a groan.

It was six o'clock, and Pat had been doing what she considered to be her one luxury: sleeping in on a weekend morning. She had always felt fortunate that the children were late risers. It was the thought of a Saturday morning with no alarm clock, and no need to get up until her body told her it was time to do so, that helped her get through her busy weekdays.

"Nathan, it's too early to get up yet. Go back to bed," she ordered, pulling the blankets over her head in hopes of getting another hour of sleep.

"Are you sure?" he asked, tugging on the blankets. "Today's the day that Gordon is going to teach me to fish. I don't want him to leave without me."

"He won't leave without you. Go back to sleep."

"But what if he does?"

By now, Pat, despite her efforts to stay sleeping, began to wonder if she was fighting a losing battle. Gordon would be there to pick them up at 8:30. If she could get Nathan to leave, she could still catch another hour of sleep.

"Nathan, if you don't let me go back to sleep, I'm going to phone Gordon and cancel the day."

As often as she tried to deny it, both to herself and to anyone around her, things between her and Gordon were moving much faster than she had anticipated. She didn't want to admit that their relationship had become an important part of her life.

They spoke on the phone every day, and her feelings for him continued to grow, but she made a point of only seeing him twice a week, three times on the odd occasion. Despite her resolution to go slow in this relationship, she found herself thinking about him constantly and anticipating the next time she would see him again.

Pat had been determined that any relationship between Gordon and her children was off limits for at least four months. He had not been allowed to participate in any family activities or spend any time with Nathan or Chelsea, other than the few minutes he was there to pick her up. She had made a conscious decision to wait until she knew if he was going to be staying in the picture before having the kids get too attached to him.

Yet somehow, Pat found herself agreeing to a picnic the previous weekend, which included all four of them spending the afternoon in the park not far from her house. She had even packed a lunch for the occasion. The park had a man-made pond, and after lunch, the four of them had rented a canoe and took a slow ride around the park. The afternoon ended with them playing catch and going back to Pat's for supper.

It was obvious from the way that Gordon got along with both Nathan and Chelsea that he had spent quite a bit of time with kids and knew how to relate to them. In the end, the day had been a huge success for everyone. Pat had watched the three of them closely throughout the day, knowing that no matter how much she enjoyed his company and no matter how much she was hoping for more of it, if he didn't get along with her children, she would not see him again.

That was the same day Gordon had promised to take Nathan fishing at Sylvan Lake in an area called Half Moon Bay, where his family owned a cabin. He told his three companions numerous stories of the many summers he had spent there as a child learning how to fish by day and then sitting around the fire pit visiting with family members and other families from neighbouring cabins by night. He explained that the cabin was not very big, but it was one of his favourite places because it held such wonderful memories.

His family also had a boat there, and he had suggested that they all go out for the weekend. The cabin had two bedrooms and plenty of room for everyone. No one from the family was using it that weekend, and he thought Nathan and Chelsea would enjoy it. Pat had declined the weekend idea but was talked into going out for the day. When Gordon told the kids about it, they were both thrilled with the idea, but Nathan was exceptionally eager to go.

Although Pat and her children had spent many weekends at their own cabin, and both kids enjoyed sitting on the pier with their fishing rods, neither one had ever been taught the art of fishing, and neither one had actually caught anything. As Gordon explained the skill of fishing to him, Nathan became eager for the weekend, imagining all the fish he was going to pull out of the water with his rod. He began talking excessively and loudly, demonstrating what he would do when the fish took his bait, and soon he was wearing on everyone's nerves. Finally Pat got to the point where she couldn't take it anymore and had to threaten him. She told him that if he didn't sit still and be quiet, he would be staying home while the rest of them went without him.

In hindsight, Pat realized that she should have warned Gordon about even suggesting future events with Nathan. At his age, a week of looking forward to a planned occasion was like an eternity, which in turn made it feel like an eternity to her too. As a general rule, she didn't tell Nathan about upcoming events any earlier than the day before.

For the past week, the first thing he would do each morning was to inform her of how many more sleeps there were until Gordon taught him how to fish. He would continue on describing, in detail, how he was going to help Gordon get the boat ready.

With all thoughts of picnics and fishing put aside, Pat shut her eyes and was soon back on the cruise ship. She was just about to take a sip from her glass when Nathan interrupted her dream once more. Realizing that there was no way she was going to be able to get him to settle down, she decided that the best thing would be to admit defeat and get up with him. It was going to be a long two hours.

Nathan ate his breakfast without Pat's usual repeated orders to quit playing and start eating. He dressed himself in record time. After that, he just sat by the living room window watching for Gordon to drive up. Every five minutes he would yell out, "Mom, how much longer? Is it just about time?"

"Nathan, if you don't quit yelling, you are going to wake you sister. It's five minutes later than the last time you asked," she would reply. "Why don't you go do something else, and then time will go faster." And you can quit distracting me, she thought.

"No, I don't want to miss him."

"You won't miss him. He'll come in and get us."

Nathan didn't budge from the window, and when Gordon showed up 15 minutes early, Pat was grateful. She thought it would calm Nathan down, but instead he got even more keyed up, constantly telling his sister and mother to hurry up before the fish were gone.

Gordon gave Pat a quick kiss and whispered, "I'll take him outside and show him the fishing gear. That should keep him out of your hair for awhile."

"Thanks, I owe you," she replied.

By the time Pat and Chelsea locked the house up and joined the boys outside, Gordon had taught Nathan the proper way to hold a fishing rod and reel in a fish, which Nathan proceeded to demonstrate for his mother and sister. If he was this attentive in the school classroom, he would be an honour student, Pat thought.

The first part of the trip to Sylvan Lake was filled with chatter and questions coming from the back seat. It was then that Pat realized how much influence Gordon had over her son in the short time they had spent together. Normally, when Nathan asked a question, he could hardly stay still long enough to hear the answer. Today, when he asked his new special friend question after question about fishing, he actually stayed quiet long enough to listen to the answers.

After 20 minutes of patiently answering all of his questions, Gordon quietly told him it was time to let the grownups talk. Nathan simply said, "Okay," then pulled out a book that Pat had brought for him to read during the trip. Chelsea, who had kept quiet the entire time, did the same.

Pat wondered how much Nathan would actually enjoy fishing. As far as she could tell, it was a sport of sit and wait, a concept that Nathan definitely had trouble with. He normally found it difficult to sit still for any length of time. The longest he had lasted fishing off the pier of their cabin was 10 minutes. After that, he just annoyed his sister, who would be perfectly content to sit with her rod in the water all afternoon, fish or no fish.

Once again, Pat pondered about her decision to let her children spend this much time with Gordon. It was true that their relationship, in her mind, was growing stronger every day, but she also knew that sometimes things just didn't work out the way one planned. She would be able to deal with a break-up, but her children had already seen their parents' marriage break up; they didn't need to see their mother fail at another relationship so soon.

What sort of an example was she setting, and how would they handle it if things didn't work out between her and Gordon? She was pretty sure he wouldn't ask for visitation rights either—he would just disappear from their lives forever.

The lake was an hour and a half drive from Calgary, and it was about an hour into the trip that Nathan finally spoke again. "Gordon, can I say something now?"

"What is it Nathan?"

"I need to go to the bathroom."

Pat and Gordon laughed. "Well, we better stop then. How about you Chelsea, do you need to stop too?"

"No, I'm fine, thank you."

Luckily there was a station just a couple minutes up the road where Gordon could pull into. "There's a restaurant here also. Why don't you girls get us a table? Nathan and I will join you in a few minutes?"

When the two did join Pat and Chelsea at the table, Nathan was still chattering away like a little chipmunk as Gordon patiently listened. Gordon smiled at Pat and sat beside her in the booth.

Nathan stood at the end of the booth, reviewing the seating arrangement. "Chelsea, why don't you go sit beside Mom so Gordon can sit here?"

"No, she's fine where she is, Nathan," Pat interjected before Chelsea could move.

Chelsea was generally the quieter of her two children, but Pat noticed that her daughter was especially quiet today. Pat made a mental note to make sure she didn't feel forgotten in the day's events. This day was about the four of them, but Pat knew that if she didn't keep control of things, the day would be about Nathan, and Chelsea would be lost in the background. As if picking up on her thoughts, Gordon reached over and placed an object in front of Chelsea.

"Nathan insists on using worms today, Chelsea, but I wasn't sure how you felt about that. I know my sister didn't like using worms when she was your age. In fact, she still doesn't. I noticed this bait when I was going by the counter just now and thought that it might be more to your liking, so I bought it for you. If you like it, we can keep it with my fishing gear, but it will be just yours. Nobody will use it but you."

Chelsea looked down at the bait lying on the table in front of her, and her eyes lit up. This day just kept getting better. Pat knew Chelsea would appreciate the fact that Gordon had bought something just for her. She looked at her Mom and then at Gordon. "Thank you," she said.

Forty-five minutes later, Gordon pulled into the driveway of his family cabin. Pat fell in love with it at first sight. The way he had described it to her, she wasn't sure what to expect. It was true that this cabin was much older than hers, but this one had more character. Standing in front of her was a rugged, one-and-a-half-story log cabin, with an open veranda wrapped around it. It had obviously been cared for over the years, and Pat could hardly wait to see the inside to see if it was as impressive as the outside.

She walked through the doorway and exclaimed, "Gordon, this is wonderful."

The logs on the outside of the cabin had been varnished to protect them from the weather, whereas the inside walls had been oiled to help keep them from drying out but kept their natural look at the same time. Straight ahead of the entry was a stairway that led to the loft above. The kitchen, dining area, and living room were actually one room, with an island dividing the three areas. Pat walked towards the rock fireplace to get a better look at it, and the views from the living room window and of the old wood-burning stove in the kitchen caught her attention at the same time. She didn't know which one to look at first.

"Gordon, it's wonderful," she repeated.

"Well, it's nothing fancy, but we like it."

Before Pat had a chance to explore any further or to relax, Nathan started tugging on Gordon's sleeve.

"Come on, let's go."

"Nathan!" Pat snapped. "You have better manners than that. Give Gordon a minute, or there won't be any fishing for you."

Nathan lowered his head. "Sorry," he said to his mother.

"It's not me you need to apologize to; it's Gordon."

"Sorry, Gordon."

"It's okay, Nathan. Why don't you come down and help me uncover the boat?"

Nathan's head snapped up, and his pout was quickly replaced with a grin from ear to ear.

"Gordon, if you want to relax for a bit, he can wait."

"Truth be known, I'm as excited as he is. Besides, it's getting late in the year, so this may be my last time out until next spring. I want to get as much time out there as I can."

"Is it okay if I go with him, Mom?" Nathan asked.

"Yes, you can go, but you listen to him and do what he says."

Gordon turned to Chelsea. "How about you, Peanut, do you want to come, too? We could use an extra pair of hands."

Pat noticed the nickname Gordon used when speaking to Chelsea. At first this act of affection pleased her; it was a sign that he was accepting her children, but immediately after, she wondered what Chelsea would think. She looked over and saw that Chelsea seemed happy to be included. Her eyes widened as she looked over to her mother for approval and before she could ask the question, Pat answered, "Go ahead, but be careful." There wasn't much need to tell her to listen to Gordon and do as he said. Brother and sister were as different as night and day.

While the three of them were busy with the boat, Pat brought everything in from the car. It took four trips and the timing was perfect. Some of the contents had been dropped off in the kitchen to be used later, and some things were put on the veranda at the back of the cabin, ready to be brought down to the boat. Just as she set the last load down on the veranda, her three companions came up to carry everything down.

Within an hour of arriving at the cabin, the four each had a rod over the side of the boat with a hook in the water. Pat had brought sweaters to protect everyone from the autumn chill, but the day had warmed, and while sitting in the boat with the sun reflecting off the lake, she found it was actually quite warm, so she allowed the children to take their sweaters off when she took her own off.

After a couple hours of fishing, it turned out that it wasn't Nathan or even Chelsea who got bored. It was Pat who wanted off the boat. Nathan and Chelsea had each caught a fish and were still riding high in the glory of it. Pat was grateful that she had been there to watch the event and see the joy on their faces as they brought the fish in with Gordon's help, but she was ready to feel the land beneath her feet again.

"Listen," she finally said, "why don't we go back and have lunch?"

"Gordon, can we cook my fish?" Chelsea quietly asked.

"Yeah, Gordon, can we cook mine, too?" Nathan jumped in before Gordon had a chance to answer.

"They haven't been cleaned, and besides, your mom made a nice picnic lunch. Maybe we should eat that instead."

"Oh," the two groaned.

"Well," piped in Nathan, "if Mom has lunch, why don't we just eat here and keep fishing?"

Pat had had enough and was grateful when Gordon came to her rescue.

"Your Mom brought lunch from home, but it's back at the cabin. I think we need to give the fish a break, so let's go in and have lunch, and then we'll come back later."

That sounded reasonable to the two young, enthusiastic fishermen, and they readily agreed—as long as Gordon promised to bring them back after lunch.

On the veranda was a table and chairs where family and friends had gathered often over the years to eat meals or play board games and cards. As soon as they got back, Pat took out the food from the refrigerator while the other three set the table outside.

Lunch was cold-cut meats, potato salad, fruit, and juice. Pat had originally placed a bottle of red wine in with the picnic lunch for the adults, but at the last minute, she had changed her mind and taken it out. There was no need to be drinking any amount of alcoholic beverage if they were going to be in the boat. Besides, as always, her first priority was to set a good example for her children.

They were barely finished eating when Nathan and Chelsea were both eager to get back on the lake. Gordon leaned over and whispered in Pat's ear, "Why don't you stay here, and the kids and I will go?"

"No, that wouldn't be fair. There are two of them and only one of you. They can be quite a handful. I know this from experience, but at least I'm used to it."

"Don't worry about me; I have plenty of experience with my nieces and nephews. Besides, they behaved great this morning. I promise you, if I have any problems we'll turn around and come right back."

Pat hesitated a moment longer, but she had to admit that he did seem to be at ease with them—and they did do as he said. The peace and quiet would be so nice, she thought. She still felt robbed of her morning's sleep.

Finally she agreed, with a little apprehension. If she hadn't been so grateful for the time alone, she would have been a little hurt when she realized that both Nathan and Chelsea seemed pleased that they didn't have to share Gordon with her that afternoon.

After they left, she put the food away and cleaned the dishes. As she tidied up, she imagined Gordon at Nathan's age and pictured him being as excited to go fishing with his dad, as her children were today. When the dishes had been put away, she found an old magazine on the coffee table and sat down on the chesterfield to read it.

The chesterfield was larger than the room required, but it didn't take long for Pat to realize that it belonged. As soon as she sat down on it, she discovered it was the most comfortable chesterfield she had ever sat on. Before long she was lying down, and within minutes she was sound asleep.

Instead of dreaming of cruise ships, this time she dreamed of Gordon as a small child running around the cabin. It was the voices from outside the cabin that woke her awhile later. She wasn't sure where she was at first, but it was Chelsea's voice that brought her back to the present. The window was opened slightly, and Pat realized that she could hear every word being said.

"Won't Mom be surprised when she finds out we caught all these fish for supper?" Chelsea asked.

"Well, if we don't get them cleaned, we might not get supper," Gordon responded. "You two sit here where you can watch what I'm doing, and I'll clean them. Maybe next summer, I can teach you how to clean them."

Pat smiled at the idea of the four of them out here next summer, and the image made her heart skip a beat. She would be happy to come back here and cook all the fish they caught, but she would leave the catching and cleaning of the fish up to them. Just as suddenly as the smile had come, it left. Maybe she should talk to him about making plans with Chelsea and Nathan that far in the future until she was sure they had a future.

Not wanting to disturb them, she decided to stay right where she was and sat up to read the magazine she had been browsing before she fell asleep. It was when she sat up and glanced out the window that she realized that not only could she hear them, but she also had a perfect view of them. She leaned back against the arm of the chesterfield to watch, undetected by the others.

Chelsea and Nathan were seated with their backs towards her and across the table from Gordon. She saw that he had newspaper spread out over the table where he was placing the parts he cut from the fish. He informed his attentive audience that those were the parts that were going to be thrown away. He explained each step of the process to them while they both sat perfectly still, with the exception of their heads which were nodding to everything he was saying.

Gordon soon looked around. From her view, it looked like he was looking for something, but didn't see it. He told the two that he would be back in a couple minutes and gave strict orders that they were not to touch anything. He then turned to leave, but before he could complete his turn, he turned back, picked up the knife, and then left with knife in hand. She couldn't see where he was going, but she took this opportunity to watch how her children behaved when left alone.

It only took ten seconds before Nathan was up off his chair and at the table where Gordon had been working. She was grateful that Gordon had thought to take the knife with him; otherwise Nathan would likely be trying to copy Gordon's actions from before.

Gingerly, Nathan lifted his hand and reached towards the fish. Chelsea said something Pat couldn't hear, and he took his hand down. It wasn't two seconds later that his little hand started to lift again. He tightly linked both hands behind his back, as if to hold them back from the temptation in front of him. His hands had a mind of their own, and he was doing his best to control them.

Pat snuggled into the back of the chesterfield with a small smile on her face as she viewed her two precious children. How could anyone who had ever sat and observed the curiosity, innocence, and very being of a child ever doubt there was a God, she thought? She truly felt that she was observing two little miracles—and to think that she had been the instrument to bring them into this world gave her a feeling of satisfaction and pride.

She was still absorbed with watching her children when the screen door to the cabin opened. It was the loud squeak of the spring holding the door to the doorjamb as it stretched that alerted her to his presence, and the sudden noise broke her solitude and startled her. Jumping at the unexpected intrusion, she dropped the long forgotten magazine to the floor. Gordon laughed, letting the screen door slam behind him.

"Didn't know you were being spied on while you were doing a little spying of your own, did you?"

"How long were you standing there?" she asked.

"Long enough to know how much pleasure you get from your children," he said. "That was a mother's smile of love and pride, if ever I saw one."

"They really are pretty good, aren't they," she stated more than asked.

"You bet they are. You're doing a great job, Pat."

"Thanks, but I haven't done it all on my own."

Then feeling the need to change the subject, she asked, "So, how many fish did you catch? It looks like a couple at least."

"We each caught three. I'm just glad Chelsea didn't catch more than Nathan. I don't know how well he would have handled his little sister catching more than him. We each threw two fish back, which really choked them both up. I told them we could only keep one each for supper, so we brought back three. They're big enough that I thought Nathan and Chelsea could share one. We're cleaning them now, as you probably already know from watching us. We should be done soon, and then I thought we could cook them over an open fire."

"You know they're each going to want to eat the fish they caught. How do you intend on getting them to share a fish that the other one caught?"

"Oh, that's all been worked out. They each get to eat the fish they caught, but they each share with you. That way, they each get half a fish, you get a whole fish, and they each get to show off to Mom. Pretty ingenious plan, don't you think?"

"Mr. Atkins, you do understand children more than I ever gave you credit for."

Just then, the screen door opened once again, and both Chelsea and Nathan came running in. Both ran over to the chesterfield sitting on either side of her.

"Mom, Mom, did Gordon tell you? We caught supper, just like in the olden days, when they didn't have grocery stores and you had to catch your own supper," Nathan said, although it came out more like a scream, something he would tend to do when he was excited.

"Nathan, keep your voice down. I'm right beside you."

"Mom," Chelsea said in a quieter tone, "Gordon said we could have supper here, if it was okay with you."

At that they both started in at the same time. "Can we, Mom? It'd be fun playing olden days. You don't even have to cook it. Gordon said he would."

Just as Pat was about to give in, she realized that fish on its own was not a meal, and she looked up at Gordon. "Well, I'm sure that would be delicious, but child cannot live on fish alone."

"No problem," he replied.

"Gordon's going to teach us how to raid a garden," Chelsea innocently added.

"I don't think so," Pat replied looking up at Gordon. "I'm not raising my children to steal."

"No, no. It's a tradition here," Gordon started.

"No. Tradition or not, it's stealing. Besides, there probably aren't any gardens still in the ground this time of year. They should have been picked by now."

Gordon laughed. "You don't understand. Every year, when I was a kid, I went over to the neighbours' yard and pulled a few vegetables. Not many, mind you, just enough to satisfy my tummy. They actually came to expect it. In fact, as I got older, I figured I should stop, but they gave me a harder time when I didn't raid the garden than when I did. Besides, now that they're a little older, I do things around the cabin for them, like hanging a new door or painting the outside of the cabin—stuff like that. They always plant more than they can eat because they enjoy gardening, but also because they feel sorry for the poor bachelor and want to feed him. They are always asking me to take some of the vegetables."

Seeing that she had the look of doubt on her face and couldn't decide whether or not to believe him, he added, "Really," just for good measure.

Gordon then spoke to Chelsea and Nathan. "Your mother is right. You shouldn't take anything that isn't yours, and this is the only garden we can ever take anything from. Actually, your mother is right about the garden being picked too. They store the vegetables in a shed until they close the cabin up Thanksgiving weekend. We won't be able to actually raid the garden until next year."

Pat caught the reference to next year again and made a mental note to talk to him about that later.

Turning back to Pat, he put one hand over his heart and raised the other as if taking an oath and asked, "If I give you my word that I really do have their permission and that I won't teach Nathan and Chelsea to steal, can I take them over there to get some vegetables, and then we'll eat here?"

"Please, Mom," Chelsea begged.

"Pleeeeeeze, Mom," Nathan added his plea, holding his hands together as if in prayer. Then, to really seal the deal, he added, "I promise to sleep in tomorrow."

Pat felt herself weakening. Besides, the thought of sleeping in tomorrow was more appealing than she wanted to admit. "We still have a long drive home. It will be late when we get home."

"We don't have to go to school tomorrow, Mom," Chelsea reminded her. "You let us stay up late on weekends."

"Okay," she gave in, "but remember; Gordon has permission to take these vegetables. He's not really stealing, and I don't ever want to hear about either one of you taking from this garden unless Gordon is with you." Then as an afterthought she added, "And I don't ever want to hear about you taking vegetables from any other garden—ever. Understood?"

With promises readily made, away they went, each one carrying a bag to fill with vegetables for supper.

Supper consisted of the fish caught earlier in the day, potatoes cut in half and seasoned with pepper and butter, and carrots done the same way with a touch of onion added. Both vegetables were double wrapped in tinfoil. Pat had prepared the vegetables with ingredients she found in the cupboards and fridge while Gordon had started a fire in the fire pit.

When Pat brought the vegetables down to the fire to be cooked, she sat next to Gordon. After poking the fire, he leaned over and whispered, "I hope you don't mind staying for supper. I know it wasn't in the plan, but after catching the fish, the kids were so excited about eating them, and I thought it would be best to cook them here. Besides, look how easy cleanup will be after."

Pat looked over and smiled. "No, I don't mind. They're pretty excited about it—and besides, I get to sleep in tomorrow. I'm pretty excited about that."

Gordon chuckled as he leaned over and gave her a quick kiss, and Pat secretly wished they were staying the weekend.

Monday, October 1

NINA SAT IN DR. WILLIS' office with her feet flat on the floor and her hands on her lap. She was studying her surroundings when Dr. Willis entered, closed the door, and sat across the desk from her patient. The doctor-patient relationship had been going on for several years, and yet this was the first time Nina had been in this office. She had been healthy her entire life, and her annual check-ups usually ended with Dr. Willis joking, "If all my patients were as healthy as you, Nina, I could go out of business."

The panic attacks had not gone away like Nina had hoped. In fact, they had started coming more often. She was having them every day now, sometimes several times a day. Although her annual check-up was not due for another month, she knew she needed help now. She was not sleeping and had become extremely edgy.

Instead of getting better the way everyone seemed to think she should, she felt herself getting weaker. Her will to carry on was leaving her, and she was falling deeper into her depression. Since her first thought of suicide in the garage two weeks earlier, she had similar thoughts at least once a day. Some days, it was just a fleeting thought; that was on the days that she considered her "good days." Other days she would spend a half-hour actually planning it. There were days when she planned it several times a day. On those days, she rejoiced at the thought.

So far, the only thing stopping her from acting on these thoughts was the thought of Mark and Jan having to deal with the loss of another parent so soon. But she didn't know how much longer that would be enough.

Choosing from the different scenarios that she had imagined, her preferred plan was when she cleaned the house so that no one would have a mess to clean up after. She would go to the garage with all doors and windows closed, sit in the car (which had also been cleaned inside and out), turn on the ignition, and simply go to sleep. She liked this one best because she would not have to endure any pain in the process, and there was no mess left behind.

After the first two nights without sleep, it felt like the panic consumed her. After the fourth, she could no longer leave her house. She was a prisoner in her own home. She realized now that she needed help.

The kids were coming home for Thanksgiving, and she didn't want them to see her like this. If she was proud of anything during this time, it was the fact that she had been able to hide from everyone just how badly she was handling her life right now. They knew that it was difficult on her (one couldn't hide everything), but nobody knew just how difficult it was. If people did, she knew they would worry, and Nina had always hated to be the cause of anyone's concern.

When she phoned the doctor's office and explained the situation, they were able to fit her in later that same afternoon. Not sure of her ability to drive anywhere, she took a taxi to the clinic. It was only because she knew that she had to do something before the kids saw her this weekend that she was able to force herself to leave the house. Well, that and a pill left over from the prescription Mark had picked up for her after Mike died. She had completely forgotten about them until she was getting ready for her appointment and she saw them in her medicine cabinet. Half an hour later, waiting for the taxi, the same surreal feeling she had during the funeral returned.

I wish I'd remembered these a lot sooner, she thought. This is neither heaven nor hell, just oh well. She grinned at her rhyme as the taxi drove up.

So, here I am, she thought, sitting across the desk from my doctor who is studying my chart. Why doesn't she say anything?

Dr. Willis looked at the test results. "Well, except for your blood pressure being a little high, which in not unusual given the circumstances, physically you are fine."

Before she could go any further, Nina jumped in. "So it's mental. Am I going crazy or having some sort of a breakdown?"

Dr. Willis sighed, placed her hands on the desk in front of her, and leaned forward. "What you are going through is more emotional than anything, but it starts a cycle. Your emotions are not allowing you to get the proper rest you need, which in turn makes you more emotional, and that in turn makes a good night sleep even more impossible. It's probably part of the reason for your blood pressure being higher than normal. You know without me telling you that when people's emotions are high or they have a lack of sleep, they don't think as clearly as they normally would.

"It's not uncommon for people to feel like this when they lose a spouse, Nina. I'm going to suggest two things. One, I'm going to renew your prescription that Mark filled for you. It should help you relax, and you should sleep better. Now, this is not a cure," Dr. Willis quickly added. "I don't want you to take these thinking that all will be fine again, because it won't.

"Let me ask you, Nina. Who in your life has been widowed?"

"My mom was."

"Is she still living?"

"No," Nina said, wondering what the doctor was getting at.

"Can you think of anyone else you know who has been widowed?"

"Not really. My aunts and uncles, but they're all gone too."

"I think what you need," Dr. Willis began as she leaned back in her chair, "is to talk to someone who really knows what you are going through. The people who care about you are probably doing everything they can to help you, but they don't really know what it is that you are feeling or dealing with.

"The second thing I am going to suggest is that you see a psychologist who I am going to refer you to. He does one-on-one counseling, but he also holds groups for people who have lost their partners to death. That way, you talk to people who can really relate to what you are feeling."

There was a moment of silence as Nina sat staring at her hands on her lap. She knew that Dr. Willis was among the people who really had no idea of what it was that she was going though. Nina knew that the doctor's husband was still alive and tonight, over coffee, they would talk about their days.

"Nina, is there anything else you want to discuss?"

"No."

"Remember what I said. These pills are not a cure. Do you want my office to set up an appointment with Dr. Anders?"

"No, that's fine."

At that point, Dr. Willis pulled open one of the desk drawers, pulled out a business card, and handed it to her patient. "Are you going to make an appointment?" she asked as Nina took the card.

Nina shrugged. Dr. Willis sighed, got up and walked around the desk. When she was standing next to her patient, she leaned back against the desk and placed her hand on Nina's shoulder.

"Nina, will you at least promise me that you will keep this card and think about it?"

"I'll think about it," Nina said, and then she walked to the door. "Thank you, Doctor."

Suddenly she didn't want to be there anymore.

As Dr. Willis opened the door, she said, "Nina, if there's anything else, please let me know."

"I will. Thank you."

Nina stopped at the drugstore in the clinic and filled the prescription. She was to take half a pill twice a day, one in the morning and one in the evening. It was advisable not to drink at all when depressed, but yes, she was allowed to have a glass of wine if she practiced moderation; no more than one at a sitting.

Nina had come to rely on her glass of wine—sometimes two—in the evening. It's not like I drink a bottle a night or drink anything stronger, she reasoned every time she thought she might be drinking too much. It's just something to calm me enough so I can get a little sleep. She usually forgot that she didn't sleep at night when she was justifying her glasses of wine.

Sunday, October 7

IT WAS THANKSGIVING WEEKEND. MARK and Jan had both arrived the day before and were leaving the next morning, so they were having their big turkey dinner on Sunday. Nina was making the stuffing when Jan joined her in the kitchen. Still sleepy-eyed, she gave her mother a kiss on the cheek and mumbled, "Mornin'," before pouring herself a cup of coffee. "Need any help?" she asked groggily, as she sat down at the table.

She asked every year, and every year her mother said the same thing, "No thanks. There's not much two people can do right now." It was always shortly before supper with the last-minute preparations that Nina would assign duties to her daughter.

In past years, while they were busy getting the meal on the table, Mark and Mike would be in front of the TV watching whatever game happened to be playing that day. If the game was an exciting one, Nina and Jan would have to speak more loudly just to be heard. Depending on how their chosen team was playing that day, Mark and Mike's cheers or criticisms could clearly be heard from the next room.

More than once, Nina asked them if they actually believed that the people on the TV could hear them. Why else would they talk directly to the coach, player, or whoever else they thought would benefit from their comments?

One year, she had asked the boys why they never helped out with the meal. There had never once been even an empty offer.

"We *are* helping, Mom," Mark had answered. "We stay out of the kitchen so we're not in your way." At that point Nina just looked over to her husband.

"Did you happen to teach him that one, or did he come up with it all by himself?"

But she never pushed the issue. It made her smile, listening to father and son enjoy their time together. Besides, she always felt that the biggest job of this meal wasn't the preparation, but the cleanup afterwards. It was Mark and Mike who took on that chore, always making sure that she didn't need to participate in that activity whatsoever, and for that she was grateful.

With the turkey in the oven now, Nina poured herself a coffee, lit a cigarette, and sat down at the table across from her daughter. "I sure am glad you both got down this weekend."

"Where else would we spend it?" Jan joked with her mother. "No one else would spoil us the way you do."

"If it keeps you coming home, I'll keep doing whatever it is I'm doing."

Neither one had said anything to her, but Nina knew her two children had worked out a schedule for coming home on the weekends. The pattern was an obvious one—Jan would come down one weekend, and then Nina would cope with the next weekend alone. Mark would come down the following weekend, and then Nina would cope with another weekend alone. Then the pattern would begin again. Nina wanted to tell them that she was fine and that they didn't need to have the schedule, but she knew that she wasn't doing fine and that she did need them.

The previous weekend had been a weekend alone, and she hadn't fared too well. It had been what finally caused her to phone the doctor Monday morning. Since the appointment, Nina had taken her pills faithfully every morning and every night. Although the heaviness was still in her chest, she did notice a difference. She was only waking up a couple times during the night, and people in general didn't irritate her as much as they had before her visit to the doctor. She was still having a glass of wine in the evening, but she made it last an hour before going to bed for the night. Nothing to concern herself about, or anyone else, she reasoned.

She had been able to get a few good night's sleep in before Jan and Mark came home and was impressed with the improvement in her appearance when she looked in the mirror. Before they arrived yesterday, she had even taken time to put some makeup on. She was convinced that there was no way they could guess the hell she had been living, so she decided that there was no need to tell them. There was also no need to tell them about the pills. The only one she had confided in was Georgia.

Over the past week, Nina had pulled out the card for the psychologist Dr. Willis had referred her to several times, only to put it back in her purse. She was convinced now that the only reason she had deteriorated to the point that she did was due to lack of sleep. She remembered Dr. Willis saying these pills were not a cure. But, Nina thought, they help me relax and sleep better, and that *is* the cure.

Things will be better now, she believed. She had even started the project that Grant had offered her. Yes, things were definitely getting better.

Because this was a special weekend, both Jan and Mark had come home. This would be the first Thanksgiving without Mike. But then, every day and every event now is a first without Mike, she thought. Nina had invited Scott and Carrie over for the day so that Mark wouldn't have to watch the game alone, and to thank them for all they had done over the past couple months. They were due to arrive at two o'clock and would stay for supper.

Jan and Nina were both still sitting at the table talking when Mark joined them, all showered and ready for the day. He poured himself a coffee and sat at the table. "If you two women make yourself gorgeous, I thought I'd take you both out for breakfast."

"What are you saying?" Jan said. "Aren't we gorgeous now?"

"Mom is," he replied.

"And I'm not? Is that what you're saying?"

"I just thought you might want to be more gorgeous than you already are, that's all."

"Yeah, right. I know what you're really saying."

"Well, I don't know if you've looked in a mirror yet today, but I think your hair might be a little extreme, even if the messy look was back in."

Nina smiled as she listened to her children banter back and forth, but she knew that if she didn't put a stop to it, it could go on for awhile.

"Mark, I've got bacon and eggs here, and the restaurants are probably busy today. I can make breakfast."

"You're going to be busy cooking all day, and this will give you a break. Plus I'm thinking of myself, Mom. If you cook breakfast, I'll have to do the dishes. Besides, the turkey will be fine for awhile."

"Come on, Mom," Jan added, "It's not often we get Mark to spend money on us. I say let's go for it."

"Hey," Mark addressed his sister, "if you don't change your attitude, Little Lady, you'll be buying your own."

It was good to have them both home, Nina thought. To a stranger it might sound like her children were fighting, but she knew they teased each other constantly, and it was music to her ears. "If it will keep peace in the family, we'll go," she laughed. "Just let me shower first."

Two hours later, after a big breakfast at a local restaurant, Nina unlocked the front door to her house. As they stepped inside the aroma of turkey greeted them. The sun shone through the windows, making the inside of the house bright, and the three of them were laughing. Nina didn't miss the fact that it was the first time since Mike's death that she had entered her own house without feeling misplaced.

She pulled the turkey out of the oven and basted it, Jan checked the messages on the answering machine, and Mark turned on the television. Nina put the turkey back in the oven and was closing the door when Jan joined her.

"Mom," Jan said, "Georgia called. She says you should call her. She's thinking of stopping by this afternoon."

"Oh, that would be nice," Nina replied. "Scott and Carrie will be here in a couple hours, and if Georgia is stopping by, why don't we get as much done for supper as we can now. Would you mind making a salad? I'll call Georgia back and then peel potatoes. I also thought we would have carrots and turnip."

Knowing there was no need to wait for a response, Nina went to find the cordless phone and call her friend back. She also grabbed her cigarettes. She hadn't had one since they left the house, because she never smoked in the car when nonsmokers were with her. It always pleased her that, although both their parents smoked, neither Mark nor Jan had picked up the habit. She knew they would like her to quit, but she had consciously decided that this was not the time; there was enough to deal with right now.

The phone was answered on the third ring. "Georgia, it's Nina. Jan said you called and were thinking of dropping by."

"I wouldn't be intruding, would I?" Georgia asked.

"Of course not. The turkey's in the oven, and Scott and Carrie are coming for supper. They'll be here in a couple hours. Why don't you stay for supper too?"

"No, thanks. I already have plans. I just thought I'd stop by and see everyone for an hour or so."

By the time Scott and Carrie arrived, Georgia was already there. Nina had been surprised when she answered the door, and beside Georgia, stood Matt.

"I hope you don't mind," Georgia said as she handed Nina a bouquet of flowers. "I stopped to pick up these flowers and ran into Matt. He hasn't been in town long, so I asked him to join me for the day."

Even if I did mind, Nina thought, what am I supposed to do? Tell you both to go away and don't come back until he's gone? Instead, she smiled and opened the door wider. "I don't mind at all," she said. "The more the merrier. Come on in."

When the doorbell rang again, Jan answered it. After saying hello to her, Scott walked through the kitchen to greet his host. Nina had heard them arrive, and as she greeted him, she handed him a cold beer and a bowl of chips.

"Mark's already in there with the TV on, if you want to join him—unless you'd rather stay here and visit with us," she offered.

"Thanks, but no thanks. I think I'd be a little outnumbered here, and besides, I can't leave poor Mark on his own."

"Yeah, right, poor Mark," the four women called in unison.

"Actually, if that's your only concern, Mark isn't alone," Georgia added. "I brought someone along, and he's in there, too."

"Well, I still think I'll join them in the other room," he said and wandered out.

Nina poured four glasses of wine and handed one to each of the women. When the other three were seated around the kitchen table, she placed a plate of pastry in the middle of the table and then joined them with an ashtray for her and Georgia to share. They had been busy catching up on each other's news when she sat down.

Georgia noticed the glass of wine and asked, "Is it okay to have alcohol with those pills?"

Jan quit talking to Carrie mid-sentence and turned to face her mother. "What pills?" she asked.

Nina had forgotten to tell Georgia that she had been the only one to share this confidential information. She hadn't anticipated a need for it; she knew Georgia would never tell anyone in the office, and it was rare that she and Jan were in the same room at the same time. Although she wasn't planning on telling anyone else, it was quite another thing to actually lie about it, especially to Jan.

"What pills, Mom?" Jan asked again.

"Sorry," Georgia said to Nina. "I didn't know it was a secret."

"Don't worry about it," Nina said, trying to make light of it. Then turning to Jan, she simply said, "The doctor renewed that prescription your brother picked up for me a couple months ago—and yes, I can have a glass of wine. I asked."

"Mom, are you okay?"

"Really, it's nothing," she reassured her daughter. "I've been having a little trouble sleeping, so I went to the doctor. She said it was normal for someone who had recently lost a spouse to not sleep well, and she thought these would help."

"Mom, I worry about you," Jan said.

I know, thought Nina. All the more reason not to tell you. Instead, she said, "Honey, I wasn't sleeping well, and it was taking a toll on how I felt, so I went to the doctor. Like I said, she says it's perfectly normal for me to feel this way, and these pills are mild. I only take half a pill at a time. I did ask the pharmacist about having a glass of wine now and then, and he said it shouldn't cause any problems. When you got here, you said yourself that I was looking better than the last time you saw me."

She leaned over and placed her hand on top of her daughter's and said, "So don't worry."

"If it was anything to worry about, you'd tell me, right?"

As far as Nina was concerned, it wasn't anything for her daughter to worry about, so she didn't feel she was lying when she answered yes.

"Jan," Carrie said. "If your mother needs anything, you know Scott and I are right next door. We'll watch her for you."

Nina was becoming irritated with this conversation and decided that it was time to end it. She was not a child that had to be babysat. She wanted to tell Carrie that she didn't need to be watched. She wanted to tell Jan not to worry about her. She was sorry she hadn't told Georgia that the conversation they'd had was not to be repeated. She looked over at Georgia, who had been quiet since getting the conversation started. Funny, she thought, you're the one that started this, and yet you haven't said a word since. Instead of saying anything to any of them, she got up from the table and went into the kitchen to baste the turkey.

When she returned, she asked Georgia, who had been looking to buy a house for several months now, how the house hunting was going. Luckily, everyone joined in on the new discussion, and the prescription pills were not brought up again that afternoon.

After Georgia and Matt left, Nina continued with the preparations for supper while Carrie and Jan set the table. Mark and Scott were still watching the game, and it must have been going the way they wanted, because the women heard several loud cheers coming from the next room. It wasn't long before it was obvious that one of the players did something Scott didn't agree with, because all of a sudden he started yelling at someone on the television.

Nina turned to Carrie, "Does he do that too? Yelling at the referees and players who have no possible way of hearing him?"

"It's a guy thing," Carrie answered simply.

The women finished getting supper on the table at the same time the game finished. Over the years, Nina had learned how to time the two together, unless there was overtime, which no one could predict. Before perfecting it, there had been the year when the food got cold while Nina waited for Mike to finish watching the game. Then there was the year when it dried out from Nina trying to keep it warm.

And, of course, there was the year she insisted on the TV being turned off so that her supper wouldn't be ruined. Without speaking a word throughout the meal, Mark and Mike had eaten so quickly that she was sure they hadn't tasted a bite of the supper she had spent hours preparing. Before Nina and Jan were finished, both men had left the table to watch the end of the game.

Today it worked out perfectly. You'd be proud of me, Mike, she thought.

When they were all sitting around the table, Nina asked Mark to say the grace. She had arranged it with him the day before, giving him time to prepare. As they all lowered their heads, he began.

"Father, we thank You for the food set before us and for the presence of those we love that we are about to share it with. We also thank You for the time You allowed us with those who are no longer with us, and for the love they gave us. We know You will look after them as they looked after us. We ask, Father, that You will continue to watch over us and guide us as You always have. Give us strength when we need it, understanding when we need it, and love always. When we think of what we don't have, please help us to appreciate that we did have it and to appreciate what we still have now. Thank You, Father. Amen."

Nina looked around at the people sitting at her dining room table. Tears filled her eyes. She raised her wineglass to make a toast but couldn't speak. They all held their glasses together. Taking her lead, they each brought their glass back to their lips and took a sip. There was a moment of silence before she spoke.

In a whispered voice she said, "Thank you all—for everything. Now let's eat before it gets cold."

Nina was conscious of the warmth that filled the house that afternoon. She had the warmth of the turkey, the warmth of the autumn sun shining through the windows and the love, and the warmth of family and friends. Later, as she was storing the leftover food, she wished that she could store some of the love and warmth of the day for when she would need it, after everyone had left.

Saturday, November 3

"Mom! It's snowing!"

Pat was still in her housecoat and was standing at her kitchen counter, making coffee. "Nathan, keep your voice down. You'll wake Chelsea."

Too excited to keep still, Nathan ran into the kitchen and grabbed his mother, almost making her spill the water she was pouring into the coffee-pot in the process.

"Nathan, it's too early for this. Settle down."

"But, Mom," he whispered, not wanting to make any noise that would wake his sister and upset his mother. "It's snowing. Big, fat flakes. I have to go out and make a snowman."

"You're not going anywhere until you've had breakfast. Besides, there was no snow on the ground when I went to bed last night, so I'm sure there's not enough snow to make a snowman yet."

"Yes, there is," he said, tugging on the sleeve of his mother's housecoat. "Come on, I'll show you."

Pat looked out the front window and was surprised to see a blanket of white snow covering everything. There was at least a couple inches on the ground, and Nathan was right that the big, fat flakes were still coming down.

"See, I told you."

"You're right, but you still can't go outside without breakfast. You get dressed and have your breakfast while I go downstairs and dig out our winter coats and boots. Then, and only then, can you go out."

Forty-five minutes later, with a steaming cup of coffee in her hand, she watched out the front window as her son rolled the first ball of snow. It was the perfect condition for building snowmen because it was a wet, heavy snow. As Nathan left his project to lie down on the ground and make a snow angel, the phone rang. Pat picked it up right away. She was enjoying her solitude and didn't want anything to wake Chelsea.

"Hello?"

"Good morning. Are you up yet?"

Right away, Pat recognized Gordon's voice. It still surprised her how just the sound of his voice made her smile.

"I am. In fact, I'm already having my first coffee."

"I was phoning to see if the kids could come out to play."

Pat laughed. "Are you only dating me for my children?"

"No. It's just one of many reasons," he teased laughingly. "Have you looked outside this morning? There's snow everywhere—and it's still coming!"

"I know. I'm sitting here looking through my window and watching Nathan build a snowman as we speak."

"Oh. Think he'd like to build a fort?"

Pat chuckled inside at the excitement in his voice. He was just a big kid in an adult's body.

"Probably, but the kids are spending the weekend with their father, remember? He's picking them up later."

"If I come over right now, would we have time to get it started?"

Pat was hesitant to agree. Jack and Gordon had already met a few times, and although they seemed to get along, she still felt uncomfortable when she was in a room with the two of them.

Just then, Chelsea entered the room rubbing her eyes. She sat down next to her mother and snuggled into her. She's just like me, Pat thought. She likes to start out slow in the morning.

Realizing that any discomfort was her issue, she replied, "Jack will be here in a couple hours. If you want to play in the snow with my kids, you'll have to come over right away."

"Okay, I'm on my way," he said and hung up.

Gordon only lived 20 minutes away, so she quickly showered and dressed, hoping to be done before he got there. She hadn't heard the doorbell ring, and as she pulled her sweater over her head, she was sure she beat him.

When she called out to Chelsea to ask if Gordon had arrived yet, there was only silence. She left her bedroom and walked through the house calling Chelsea's name, but there was no response. She was getting concerned when she got to the living room and looked out the window. There, in her front yard were Gordon and Chelsea helping Nathan build his snowman.

Before Nathan had gone outside, Pat had retrieved all their winter clothes from storage in the basement. Deciding to join in on the fun, Pat pulled her boots, coat, toque, and mitts from the front closet.

Wanting to sneak up on them, she went out the back door so they wouldn't see her. As she stepped out, the brisk fresh air hit her and brought more to her bounce than any morning coffee could. Going around the side of the house, she hid behind the corner of the house and made a snowball. When she was sure no one was looking, she took aim and threw it straight at Gordon. Her aim was perfect, but a split second before the snowball reached him, he bent over to pick up more snow to pack on the snowman, and it went over his head. When it landed on the ground next to him, he stood up and looked around.

"Did you kids throw that?" he asked, looking where the snowball had landed.

"No," they replied together.

"Chelsea, did you say your mother was in the shower?"

"She was when I came out."

Pat picked up another handful of snow and packed it into a ball. She peeked around the corner to get a better view of her target, but Nathan was looking in that direction and saw her. She tried to signal him to keep her whereabouts a secret when he yelled, "Gordon! There she is."

Gordon reached down and came up with his own handful of snow. As he was busy packing his snowball, she took the opportunity to throw hers. It got him in the shoulder. She hadn't finished rejoicing in her success when she got one on the head.

"Hey!" she cried out.

"Well, you started it," was all he had to say.

She picked up another handful of snow and formed it into a ball. She had no sooner thrown it when she got hit with another, and then again. The last one didn't quite make its destination, landing at her feet instead.

"This isn't fair," she disputed. "It's three against one."

"If you admit defeat and play nice, we'll quit. Right, team?"

"Right!" Chelsea enthusiastically agreed.

Nathan looked up at Gordon. "Do we have to?"

"Yeah, I think we'd better. You guys will be safe at your dad's later, but I could pay for this for the rest of the day."

Nathan thought about it for a few seconds. "Right," he said.

"Do you admit defeat?" Gordon asked.

"I admit outnumbered."

Getting ready to throw another snowball, Gordon asked again, "You are the one that started it with a sneak attack. Now, do you admit defeat?"

Knowing what would follow if she didn't admit defeat, she said, "All right, all right. I admit defeat, but only because I was outnumbered."

"Spoken like a true sore loser."

The four of them spent the next hour finishing the snowman, complete with carrot nose, raisin eyes, and buttons. When the kids wanted to top it off with a hat and scarf, Pat went back to the basement. She had a box full of old winter clothes ready to be given away. In the box she was able to find a hat and scarf to fit the snowman. When she joined them again, she saw that they had found a couple of dead branches somewhere and used them for arms.

Admiring their work, it was Chelsea who came up with the idea that if they each made a snow angel around the snowman, the angels would protect it. They were all on the ground waving their arms and legs when a car pulled into the driveway. Pat looked up and recognized Jack's car.

"Dad!" the kids called as they ran towards it. Pat walked to the car to greet him.

"Jack, I'm sorry. I guess I lost track of time. Their bags are just about packed. I can have it done in five minutes, but I think they'd better change into dry clothes. Why don't you come in for a cup of coffee?"

"No problem," he replied. "It looks like everyone was having fun." Jack held his hand out and shook hands with Gordon. "How's it going, Gordon?"

"Pretty good. Yourself?"

"Can't complain."

Jack had confessed to Pat just days before that he liked her new boyfriend, but that he was still adjusting to the idea of someone else with her instead of him. Pat wasn't sure she would have been as graceful, had the roles been reversed.

Looking back at Pat, he asked, "Do you still keep the sliders in the garage?"

"They're exactly where they've always been. Did you need them?"

"Well, I thought maybe the kids and I would see if we could find a hill that's not too busy this afternoon and make a few trips down it."

Chelsea and Nathan were on either side of Jack. When they heard the plans for the afternoon, they were anxious to get going right away.

"Not yet," he informed them. "You heard your mother. Go inside and get some dry clothes on. Then he told Pat, "If you want to finish their packing while they change, I'll find the sliders and then come in."

Both Chelsea and Nathan had run inside to change so they could leave for the weekend with their father. Pat found only a heap of snow clothes on the floor when she and Gordon entered the house. She picked them up, brought them to the laundry room, and put them in the dryer before she finished the packing. Gordon, who was becoming familiar with the household, went straight to the kitchen to make some fresh coffee.

After putting the sliders in the trunk of his car, Jack stayed for a cup of coffee while the clothes finished drying. With the clothes dry and his coffee gone, he and the kids left. Pat hugged both her children and watched them leave. It always struck her as strange that every time she watched the three of them leave, she wondered how it was that they had messed up so badly that it had come to this, even though the breakup was her idea.

Gordon walked up behind her and put his arms around her. "Miss them already, don't you?" he asked.

"Yeah. Silly, isn't it? I look forward to the peace and quiet, and yet every time they leave, all I look forward to is their return."

Gordon gave her a little kiss on the neck. "Well, let me see if I can make you feel better."

Pat turned around and put her arms around him. He ran his finger along her jaw line and gazed into her eyes. "I'm so lucky to have found you," he said before slowly leaning down and covering her mouth with his own. She responded and tightened her arms around him, holding herself closer to him.

It was then that her stomach began to growl, making a most unromantic sound in a romantic moment. Gordon pulled away and looked down. Pat couldn't help herself, and she began to laugh. "Oops," was all she got out.

"Maybe I'd better take you out and feed you," he said.

He brought her to a restaurant in a mall so he could do some shopping. "I need some new winter clothes," he explained. "I just didn't think I would need them this soon."

The mall wasn't busy, so they browsed all the stores as they went along. By mid-afternoon, Gordon had bought a jacket for himself, and Pat had bought gloves for herself and a book for each of the kids. When they were passing a jewelry store, out of habit Pat slowed her pace to look in the display case. Gordon followed her lead and slowed down with her.

"I don't even know what kind of jewelry you like," he said. "What do you think of those?" he asked, pointing out a gold chain with a solid gold bird pennant.

"Oh, that's different," she said. "It's simple and yet very eye-catching at the same time. I like that."

"Oh! Look at that!" She exclaimed, as she pointed to the necklace beside it.

"The lady has expensive tastes, methinks," Gordon said with a laugh, studying the string of diamonds and sapphires.

It was then that the sales clerk who had been watching them decided to approach. "Isn't that lovely? These are the matching earrings to go with it." She opened the display case bringing out the necklace and a pair of earrings shaped into the form of a leaf made entirely of diamonds and sapphires.

"Would you like to try the necklace on?" she asked.

"No thanks. It's lovely, but I'd only get the opportunity to wear it a few times during the year, at most. Besides, I think they're a little out of my price range."

"Thanks, anyway," Gordon said to the sales clerk as they moved along. "I think we'll just keep window shopping."

They continued to take their time as they passed different pieces of jewelry. Gordon would pick something out to get Pat's opinion on it. When they got to the engagement rings, he continued to point out different items and seemed surprised at her simple tastes: the bigger the piece, the more she shied away from it.

"I know it's a lovely piece, and on someone else, it would be beautiful. I just can't see myself wearing something like that." She was about to turn away so they could carry on to other stores when something caught her eye, and she couldn't help but stop and take a closer look.

"Now that is beautiful without being too outspoken."

Gordon looked to where she was pointing. It was an engagement ring with a larger diamond in the middle and a smaller one on either side. He had to admit that it was a ring that would suit her. He also had to admit that she was right in the fact that it was beautiful without being too gaudy.

The rest of the afternoon was spent wandering through a few more stores, and then they drove down Memorial Drive. They stopped the vehicle, and strolled down the path along Bow River. By now the snow had stopped, and everything was softly covered in white. With the sun shining down, the ground sparkled like small diamonds, and clumps of snow dropped from the trees as the heat of the afternoon sun melted the snow off the branches.

Pat had put a roast in the oven and set the timer before they left. It was four o'clock now, and she wanted to get home soon to place the small potatoes around it, which would cook while she made salad. With the shorter days of the season, it was already getting dark by the time they returned back to her home. They entered the house, and the aroma of the roast greeted them before they found the light switch.

"You know," Gordon said, as he took off his jacket, "there's something about coming in from the dark and cold into a bright, warm house with the smell of a good meal to greet you. You just can't help but feel good, can you?"

"You're right," Pat replied. To herself, she thought, it helps to walk in with someone you care about too. But she said nothing as she took off her own coat.

After supper, while sitting in front of the fireplace drinking cognac, Gordon leaned back and put his arm around Pat.

"Did you enjoy yourself today?" he asked.

"Very much."

"Me too." At that he turned and faced her. "Do you want to know what I enjoyed most about today?"

"What?"

"I really love being with you, Pat. You're so much fun to be with. We laugh a lot and never seem to run out of things to talk about. When I'm not with you, I find myself looking forward to the next time that I can be."

Pat sat quietly. He reached over and gently caressed her cheek. She looked up, gazed into his eyes, and smiled.

"I love our time together too, Gordon."

He hesitated a moment, but just a moment. Finally, he said, "I love you."

Friday, December 21

CHRISTMAS WAS ONLY FOUR DAYS away. Mark and Jan would be there early afternoon the next day. Nina looked outside at the snow coming down and silently hoped that the roads would be good for her children to travel on. At one time, she would have said a silent prayer, but she hadn't talked to God for months. As far as she was concerned, He didn't listen anyway.

She picked up her glass of scotch and took a sip before returning to the chore in front of her. It was already eight o'clock in the evening, and she still had a lot to do before going to bed that night. She had been trying to wrap gifts for the past hour and so far had only accomplished wrapping a sweater for Jan.

After Thanksgiving, her depression had lifted somewhat. She took her medication faithfully and got out of the house more often. Knowing how tight her deadline had been, she committed herself to working on the office project every day until it was finally finished three weeks earlier, right on schedule. Sometimes she had worked from the office, but mostly she worked from home.

She preferred working from home because of the cramped quarters in the office. Matt had offered to move out of her old office, but she didn't think that made sense and refused his offer. She still wasn't ready to commit to coming into the office every day, so she set up a temporary working station in an unoccupied cubicle, which she used only when it was necessary to work from the office. The rest of the time she had her papers spread out in the den at home.

Working from home not only meant that she had more room, but it also meant that she could work the hours she wanted. In the middle of the night when she was restless and sleep would not come, which was most nights, she would work on the project for hours. The pills were helping her get more sleep than she had been getting before seeing Dr. Willis, but she still hadn't slept through a night, and there were nights when even the pills didn't help. On those nights, when most people were getting up to start their day, she was just going to bed.

She didn't know if Grant was more pleased or surprised that she had actually finished the project on time. It was after the project was completed that the depression began to set in again. During the first week, she convinced herself that it was because she had too many hours to fill, and she decided to give Grant a call telling him she was ready to come back—at least part time—but somehow she never made the phone call.

Depression had started to take over again, wrapping around her like an invisible blanket. Over the course of the past three weeks, days would go by without Nina getting dressed. Unless she was expecting someone, she sat around all day in her housecoat. On those days, if someone did unexpectedly come to the door, she would sit quietly in her chair waiting for whoever was standing at her doorstep to go away.

She even started letting the answering machine screen her calls for her. When Nina did return calls, it was always at a time when she was able to put on the charade of a woman getting on with her life. She had started having success convincing her children that she was doing much better, and they were coming home less often. She knew it was time they quit worrying about her and got on with their own lives—even if she wasn't able to.

She was dreading the next two weeks and had been for some time now. Lighting another cigarette, she remembered Christmases past as she took another sip of her scotch. She put the glass down next to a small box, slowly picked the box up, and held it close. After a moment she opened it hesitantly.

Christmas had always been her favourite time of year. Every year she would fight the crowds on Boxing Day to purchase decorations and wrapping paper for the following year. Throughout the year, she always kept her eyes open for special gifts for each person on her list. When she found them, she bought them and attached a small paper with the name of the intended recipient; then she would put it in a large box in the basement that was kept for the sole purpose of holding her secret purchases. She doubted that she would ever look forward to Christmas again. This year the season seemed to creep up on her and catch her unprepared.

Mike knew about the box, but he swore to her that he never peeked in it, and she believed him. Unwrapping the gift Christmas morning to see what it was that she had unearthed for him meant as much to him as watching his expression when he opened his gift meant to her. A week before Christmas, she always got the box out to take inventory and to start wrapping. Sometimes the names got changed, but always there were last-minute shopping sprees for at least one person who didn't have as many gifts in the box as everyone else.

Nina looked at the Swiss knife that was contained in the small box she held in her hand. Early last summer, Mike and Nina has taken the motor home on a road trip for two weeks. They stopped at different campgrounds along the way, sometimes staying only one night, sometimes as many as three.

During one of their stops, they had driven into Canmore, a small community not far from their campsite. They strolled down the streets and stopped in several quaint local stores that held items unique to the area. It was at one of these stores that Mike found the pocketknife.

Looking back now, Nina remembered Mike's reaction when he spotted the knife. His actions and the enthusiasm of his discovery reminded her of a small child who had just discovered a new toy.

"Look at this, Hon," he had said, opening each tool attached to show her. "When I was a kid, I always wanted one of these. This would be so useful, too, especially when we're camping. Look, it's got a knife, a screwdriver, and a small pair of scissors."

Just then the sale clerk came over. "That's a beautiful knife, sir. Should I ring it up for you?"

"How much is it?" Mike asked.

"That one you have there is a very fine knife. Look at the mother-of-pearl handle. Isn't it a beautiful piece? This particular knife has everything you should ever need if you're ever stranded, and the quality is outstanding. As long as you take care of it, this knife should do you the rest of your life."

"How much is it?" Mike repeated.

"Well, you would have to look hard to find another one better. That's why the asking price on this particular knife is $150."

Mike handed it back to the sales clerk. "No thanks."

"Are you sure, sir? You seem like the kind of man who has probably seen a few of these knives in his time. Have you ever seen one nicer?"

"No thanks," was all Mike said, and he walked away.

Nina followed. Outside the store, she questioned him about it. "Why didn't you buy it? You seemed to really like it."

"It seems silly to pay that kind of money for something I don't really need. It would be nice to have, but realistically we already have everything on that knife in the motor home already."

"Michael Vincent Andrews," she said, using his full name, and she stopped right there in the middle of the street to scold him. "You love that knife, and we have reached a point in our lives where that should be enough reason to buy it. It's $150, not $150,000."

"Nina, it's not practical to pay that much for something I don't really need. Besides, I didn't like that sales clerk, he was too much of a...a salesman. Somehow, I just didn't trust him," he said before continuing down the street, indicating that the conversation was over.

Nina wanted to continue the conversation but knew it would be pointless. Instead, when Mike found a sports store he wanted to roam, she told him that she would be bored in there and wanted to explore some of the other quaint stores they had not yet ventured into. They decided to each go their separate way and agreed to meet at a local restaurant in one hour.

Five minutes later, Nina was holding the knife in her hand. "My husband really liked this knife, but he thought the price was too much. I want to buy it for him for Christmas, but is there any way you can drop the price?"

"Madame, your husband is very lucky to have a wife like you. Take another look at the knife. With that kind of workmanship, this is very find quality. He will never have a problem with this knife. And you would have to look a long time before finding all these particular tools on another knife."

Nina agreed with Mike. She didn't care for this salesclerk either, but she knew that Mike had really liked this knife.

Ten minutes later, she stood outside the store with the knife in the small box she held in her hands now. She had paid $120 and was proud of herself for getting the price down. She just wished she could share her story with Mike, but that would have to wait until Christmas morning after he had opened it.

Nina placed the small opened box back down on the table where she could see the knife, and she regretted that she would never be able to share that story with him. She picked up her glass of scotch and wondered once again how she was going to make it through the next two weeks. "Dear God," she silently prayed, "I don't know if You listen to me anymore, but I need a miracle."

Nina's prayer never went any further. In her opinion, there was no need to continue trying to communicate with God. He obviously quit listening to me awhile ago, she thought. If He hadn't, Mike would be with me today, and I wouldn't be wondering what purpose life had for me anymore. For now, I had better just try to get as much done as possible before the kids get here tomorrow and then carry on the best way I know how.

With a sigh, Nina took another sip of scotch, realized her glass was empty, and got up to pour another. What she didn't realize was how much she had come to rely on her evening cocktails to help her get through the nights.

Putting her refilled glass back down on the table, she picked up the next gift to wrap. It was a book on house maintenance and projects for Mark. He had bought a fixer-upper house in the spring and was attempting to do as much of the work as he could on his own. Hopefully, this would come in handy.

Monday, December 24

FOR CHRISTMAS EVE, THE ANDREWS' house was full of friends. Among them were Scott and Carrie, plus Georgia, who brought Matt with her again. Nina had met Matt a few times now, and she found that she actually enjoyed his company. Nina noticed that whenever he was in the room, her anger disappeared, and she was more at peace with the world.

It made absolutely no sense to her why he had this effect on her. It didn't seem to be anything in particular that he said or did, but she had come realize that if he was near, even in a crowded room, she knew she would be free of any anxiety attack that day.

Grant and his wife, Janet, stopped by for a couple of hours, and Mark and Jan each had over friends with which they had grown up. Nina listened to the laughter and looked around the room. She estimated there were 20 people in her home. Because everything in her life was still categorized as "before Mike died" and "since Mike died," she made a mental note of the fact that this was the most people she'd had in her house since the small party they'd had the night before they brought Mike to the hospital. That would put this night into the "since Mike died" category.

Matt walked over to where Nina was standing and stood beside her. "Thanks for letting me come, Nina. I'm really enjoying myself."

"I'm glad you could come," she said, knowing that she really meant it. "Can I get you anything, a drink or a plate of nibbles?"

"No, thanks. I think I'll be going. It looks like you got a house full of people who care about you. It's good to hear laughter, isn't it?"

"Yes, it is," she answered simply.

"It's good to remember these times too, Nina," he added. "Good memories are like a blanket. Just like a blanket will warm you when you are cold, a happy memory can help warm your heart when you're sad."

Nina looked at him, trying to figure him out. She had never met anyone like him before. She was wondering how to respond when he placed his hand on her shoulder.

"Merry Christmas, Nina," he said. "I'm going to leave now. I'll see myself out so you can attend to your guests." Nina watched him closely as he left the room.

Everyone was gone by eleven o'clock, and Nina started picking up the dirty dishes shortly after. Mark and Jan pitched in, and the job was done in half an hour. By midnight, Nina had said good night to Mark and Jan and was in bed. The tears fell silently as she cried herself to sleep.

Monday, December 31

BOTH MARK AND JAN WERE home for 11 days. Jan's school was on Christmas break for two weeks, and Mark had taken vacation days from work. The time was filled with visitors, phone calls, and laughter—lots of laughter. When the three of them had quiet time, they pulled out the games and movies like they did every year for as far back as Mark and Jan could remember. There was bowls of popcorn, baking, turkey, and food galore.

Mark and Jan went out with friends a few times, and on those occasions, Nina found the house so big and lonely. She dreaded the day they would leave. Both were still home for New Year's Eve, and Nina knew they had been invited to a few parties. She convinced them both that she was tired and would actually enjoy a quiet evening.

She rented a movie, opened a bottle of red wine, and made a bowl of popcorn. By midnight, she was sound asleep.

~~~~~~~~~~~~~~~~~~~

Pat put on the earrings that Gordon had given her for Christmas, and then she stood back and looked at herself in the full-length mirror. The earrings were the same ones she had seen in the store with him months earlier. She had thought they were too expensive for something she would only wear a few times a year, but apparently he hadn't.

When she opened the small box on Christmas morning, her only reaction was to sit and stare, speechless. Because she had seen them in the store, she knew how much they cost. She thought it was too much and told him so. He insisted that it was his money, and until it was their money, he could spend it any way he wanted.

It wasn't until later, while stuffing the turkey, that the words "until it was their money" came back to her. What did he mean by that? Was he saying that she should back off because she has no say? After all, he was right—it was his money, and she had no say. Or was he saying that he was thinking of taking their relationship to another level, and that one day they would have joint assets, so it would be "their money"? Pat tried not to think about it.

She had spent a day Christmas shopping with him and had helped him pick a few gifts out for Chelsea and Nathan. While he had been busy looking at expensive gifts for them, she was constantly explaining to him, "I don't want spoiled children," and then pointing out less expensive gifts. When the gifts were opened Christmas morning, she realized that he had purchased a couple extra gifts without her knowledge. It may be his money, and the extra gifts may not have cost as much as he initially wanted to spend, but they were her children, and she truly did not want them spoiled. She decided that later, when Chelsea and Nathan were with their father, she would explain this to him again.

That had been a week ago, and tonight was New Year's Eve. Pat had been lucky enough to find a babysitter. Because she hadn't planned on going out, she never booked Kelly, and her babysitter had made other plans. While she was making her tenth phone call, she was about to admit defeat when Nancy came into her office.

"I wasn't trying to eavesdrop, but are you looking for a babysitter for New Year's Eve?"

"Yes. Do you know of any?"

"How about me?"

"Don't you have any plans?"

"No, just me and the TV. I can do that at your place."

"Nancy, are you sure? I really appreciate the offer, but it's an awful lot to ask."

"You didn't ask; I volunteered." Apparently Pat didn't look convinced, so Nancy continued. "Pat, you haven't been happy for so long, but since you met Gordon, you've been your old self again. I really don't have plans, and I want to do it. Besides, maybe I'm doing it for myself. You're a lot more fun to be around since you met Gordon, and if I have to be with you every day, I want to do my part to help keep him around."

Pat laughed. "I wasn't the best person to be around for awhile, was I?"

"Don't worry about it; you had a lot on your plate. I'm just happy to see you happy again."

"I really am, you know."

"I know," was all her assistant said before leaving the room.

Pat had rented two movies that night, one the kids would enjoy and one that Nancy could enjoy after the kids were in bed. She was putting treats out when the doorbell rang. Chelsea, who had recently elected herself for the position of greeting person, always ran to be the first one to answer the door or phone, and this time was no exception.

"I'll get, I'll get it," she called, running towards the door.

Pat continued with what she was doing, secretly pleased that Chelsea had taken on this responsibility.

Nancy came into the kitchen, letting her presence be known to Pat. "Wow, have plans changed and we're having a party here tonight?" she asked, looking at all the food on the counter.

"No, Smarty, I just appreciate you doing this for me, and I don't want you to be sorry for offering your services. Besides, you never know when I might need to call on you again."

"Anytime," she replied, just as the doorbell rang again. "I believe your Prince Charming has arrived."

Gordon's first comment when he entered the kitchen was the same as Nancy's had been just minutes before. "Wow!" Pat wondered if his comment was towards the food, as Nancy's has been, and then she noticed that his line of vision was on her. Pat never noticed Nancy quietly leave the room.

"Lady, you are absolutely gorgeous," he exclaimed as he reached out for Pat's hands and held them, greeting her with a kiss. Still holding her hands, he took one step back and slowly took in every inch of her. His eyes rested on the earrings delicately hanging from her ears. His hands reached up and gently brushed the jewels. "I'm so glad you wore these. Seeing them on you makes them even more beautiful." Crossing his arms and cupping his chin in his hand, as if trying to solve a problem, Gordon took another step back. "Something isn't right," he said.

Pat had been pleased with her reflection in the mirror earlier and with his reaction, but now she was suddenly concerned. Just as she was thinking of leaving to recheck her hair, he seemed to come up with the solution.

"I've got it!" he exclaimed. "As beautiful as those earrings are, they just don't seem complete without this." Reaching into his pocket, he pulled out a long, black box and held it open towards her.

Pat's eyes widened as she stared, speechless—much the same reaction as Christmas morning, when she had opened the small box that contained her earrings. In the box he held in front of her now was the matching necklace to the earrings she wore. "Gordon," was all she managed to whisper.

"Do you like it?"

"Omigosh. I love it."

Gordon put the box down on the counter and proceeded to remove the necklace from the box. He directed her, "Turn around so we can see how it looks."

Pat did as she was told. Her hand instinctively went up to touch the jewels around her neck as he secured the clasp. When he was done, he gave her a small kiss at the nape of her neck, and it sent shivers through her. He placed his hands gently on her shoulders and turned her around so that he could see the completed picture.

Satisfied with what he saw, he wrapped his arms around her and held her close. Pat held him tight, determined not to cry for fear of ruining her makeup.

"Thank you. It's beautiful."

"You deserve beautiful things. I hope I can always give them to you. You make me happier than I have ever been. I love you."

"I love you too."

Gordon's hands cupped her face, and he looked into her eyes before leaning down to kiss her. It started out slow, and then as it grew deeper, he pulled her to him.

Pat returned his kiss, leaning into him and wanting him as close as possible. His hand moved up and caressed her neck. Then with the realization of the others in the next room, he stepped back.

"Woman, sometimes you make me forget that there's anyone else in the world. Maybe we should get going before we get caught."

"Okay," was all she could manage as she turned to lead the way out of the kitchen.

"Unless you want me to give them $20 to go out for pizza, and we can have the place to ourselves for awhile," he whispered, half-joking.

"Don't tempt me," she whispered back, half-serious.

After the appropriate "oohs" and "aahs" from the others as they looked at the necklace, Gordon and Pat were in the taxi and on their way to the New Year's Eve celebration at one of the downtown hotels. When Gordon had said they were taking a taxi instead of driving, Pat had agreed that it was a good idea; that way he wouldn't have to worry about how many drinks he had before the drive home.

"Oh, yeah, that too," he had replied. "I just thought it would give us extra snuggle time in the back seat."

When they arrived at the hotel, they found the room in which the celebration was being held. The room held approximately 450 people and was beautifully decorated with balloons, streamers, and paper bells. Their ticket included a meal of roast beef, Yorkshire pudding, mashed potatoes, vegetables, a salad, and dessert. After the meal, a live band would perform, and there would be dancing; then, just before midnight, each table would receive a bottle of champagne to toast the New Year.

They were meeting two other couples and found one of them already sitting at the table. Pat sat next to Claire. The two women had only met a couple of times before but had hit it off immediately. Her husband, Dave, and Gordon had been close friends for years.

"In fact," Dave had told her the first time they met, "that fellow you're with was best man at our wedding. If he ever decides to settle down, I owe him a thing or two. Let's see if his bride thinks the little pranks are any funnier than mine did."

"Why do you think I've never settled down?" Gordon had joked.

"You better be afraid, my friend," Dave had replied. "Be very afraid."

Gordon and Dave went for drinks. It wasn't long after they returned to the table that the other couple arrived. The entire evening, in Pat's opinion, was wonderful. The meal was delicious, the band was great, and she enjoyed the company she was with immensely.

When they finally arrived back at her place, Pat took her shoes off and realized that she may have enjoyed the band too much. She had danced twice with Dave, but it was Gordon who had her on the dance floor for most of the evening.

"You know, they say you should watch what you wish for, because you just might get it. I think I know what they mean now," she said, placing her shoes in the closet.

"What did you wish for?" he asked.

"A man who liked dancing."

Gordon walked up behind her and put his arms around her. "Are you saying that you're sorry you met me?" he joked.

"No." She turned to face him and put her arms around him. "You just have to take me out dancing more often so my feet get used to it."

"You've got yourself a deal," he laughed and kissed her nose. "Why don't you go check on the kids, because I know you won't relax until you do. I'll go say hello to Nancy, and when you get back I'll massage your feet."

"You've got yourself a deal."

Both Chelsea and Nathan were sleeping, Nathan in his own bed and Chelsea in Pat's. When Nancy and Pat were making plans for the evening, both had agreed that it would probably be best for Nancy to spend the night. Chelsea would sleep with Pat, and Nancy would sleep in Chelsea's bed. That way Nancy didn't have to worry about the traffic, and if Pat was late coming home, she could just go to bed when she was tired. Pat did arrive home later than anticipated, but she wasn't surprised when Nancy was still up and waiting.

Both Nathan and Chelsea had kicked off their covers, so Pat pulled the blankets up and gave them each a kiss on the forehead. They really are angels, she thought. She knew she was blessed for having them.

When she entered the living room, Nancy and Gordon were comparing their evenings, each of them certain that theirs was the more enjoyable. Pat joined Gordon on the couch, leaning back and putting her feet on his lap.

"I guess this is for the massage I promised you," Gordon noted.

"A promise is a promise."

Gordon massaged her feet while the three visited. It was a perfect ending to a perfect evening, until Gordon picked up her feet, placed them on the floor, and announced, "Well, I have to get going. I'm not going to bother calling a taxi; I'll just take my car."

Nancy stood up, "I think I'll head to bed. Goodnight."

Pat walked Gordon to the door. He gave her a kiss and held her. "Thank you for bringing in the New Year with me. I hope this year is as good as the last year ended."

"Me, too," she replied, holding him tight.

Saturday, January 5

WHEN THE DOORBELL RANG, CHELSEA jumped up and ran down the hall, her feet barely touching the floor. "I'll get it! I'll get it!" she yelled.

Of course you will, Pat thought. Who else would have a chance? Right behind her was Nathan. "Me too! Me too!"

Jack was picking them up to spend the rest of the weekend with him, and a distinctive trait of his was to either arrive right on time or five minutes early. Generally, it was the latter. Pat used to joke with him that if he was ever ten minutes late, she would call out the coast guard to go searching for him. Today, he was right on time.

She heard his voice at the door and stood up from the kitchen table where the four of them had been playing games. "Well, I guess we'll finish this game another time," she said to Gordon as she left the room to greet Jack.

"I'll put the cards away, and then come say hello," he replied.

A blizzard had started, and Pat could feel the cold air in the hallway from the door having been opened.

"It looks like it's getting pretty bad out there. How are the roads?" she asked Jack.

"Not bad yet, but I think we should get going soon before they get any worse. I don't imagine we'll be venturing out too far today."

"We can teach you a new card game we learned today, Daddy," Chelsea offered.

"Yeah," followed Nathan.

"Well, they're all packed and the bags are right here," Pat said. "You kids make sure you're bundled up tight. Don't forget your toque and scarf. Nathan, you make sure you wear your mitts today, and don't stuff them in your pocket like you normally do."

"Yes, Mom," he replied, rolling his eyes.

Pat was about to say something to him when Gordon joined the group. He walked up to Jack and held out his hand, "Happy New Year, Jack."

Jack took Gordon's hand and shook it. "And the same to you. Well, if you kids are ready, let's get going."

Snow blew in when he opened the door to leave, letting them know that the weather was getting worse by the minute. "Be careful," Pat said. Then as an afterthought, she added, "Jack, would you mind calling when you get back to your place, just so I won't worry?"

"Will do," he called back, running down the stairs to his car for protection against the elements.

When the door closed, Gordon stood perfectly still and said, "Listen."

Pat listened, but could hear nothing. "What do you hear?" she asked.

"Silence."

"It sounds nice now, but you wait, after awhile it becomes deafening."

"I know," he laughed. "I hope you know that I'm just joking. Chelsea and Nathan are great kids, and I've come to love them very much."

"I know and I'm glad. If you didn't get along with them, I'd have to let you go."

"Then I better make sure we get along," he said as he put his arm around her. "I don't plan on giving you any reason to let me go. What I should do, though, is go home and change for dinner tonight. Our reservations are at seven, and it's four-thirty now. If the roads are getting as bad as Jack says, I might need a little extra time."

Pat hesitated and then asked, "Would you be terribly disappointed if we cancelled our reservations, ordered in pizza, and watched movies? There's been so much going on for the past month, it would be nice to just stay home."

"Well, I was hoping to make it a special evening, since we haven't had much time alone, but if you want to stay here, that suits me just fine."

"Are you sure you won't mind? I know you made the reservations awhile ago, and you were counting on going out, but it would be nice to just sit at home with our feet on the couch, watch an old movie, eat pizza and popcorn, and maybe have a beer. Besides, I'm not sure we want to be on the roads tonight."

"Well, when you put it that way, I don't even want to go out."

"Great!" she said. "You go order pizza, and I'll find a couple movies."

"Sounds like a plan."

Pat went to the cabinet that held her movies, and Gordon headed for the phone, first to cancel their reservations and then to order pizza. Pat ran her finger across the titles of movies, hoping to touch one that jumped out and said, "Watch me." She knew she had her old favourites, like *Sleepless in Seattle* and *Regarding Henry*, but she wasn't really sure that Gordon would appreciate them.

She decided to get his opinion and turned to call him. "Gor—" was all she got out before he entered the room. "Oh. Hi. I was just about to ask you to come help me pick out a movie. What kind of movie are you in for the mood for? I've got quite a selection from animated like *Lady and* the Tramp and *Cinderella*, to westerns like *Silverado* and a couple John Wayne movies. I've got romantic like *Sleepless in Seattle* and comedy like *The Whole Nine Yards*. Well, you look. What would you like to see?"

"It doesn't matter. What would you like to see?"

"I'm not sure; that's why I called you."

"Okay, this could go on all night, and we won't see anything. Let me put it this way. If you were home alone and decided to watch a movie, what movie would you pick? I'll let you know if I want to see it."

"If I were home all alone, I would probably curl up on the couch and watch *Sleepless in Seattle*, but it's a romantic movie and always makes me cry, so I'm not sure you'd like to see it. Same question to you—If you were here all alone and decided to watch a movie, what movie would you pick?"

"Well, hold on. You're just assuming that I don't want to see *Sleepless in Seattle*. I've never seen it, but I've heard some really good things about it."

"Yeah, from who?"

"Claire."

"There you go, another woman's opinion. What did Davie say about it?"

"Surprisingly, he thought it was good too. Why don't we watch it, and if I don't like it, I get to pick the next two movies we watch?"

Pat hesitated. Even though it was a romantic, she knew a few men who really enjoyed the movie. If he didn't like it though, she wasn't sure what movies he would pick. What if they were sci-fi or horror? She hated both of those. Well, sometimes you just had to take a chance.

"You're on," she said.

"Great, then let's take the movie into the living room and decide on what kind of pizza to order."

"I thought you did that."

"Apparently I'm no better at picking out pizza than you are at movies."

Just then the phone rang. "Well, I'm guessing that's not the pizza man to say the pizza is ready."

Pat ran to the kitchen. Recognizing the number on call display, she picked up the receiver. "Hello, Jack? Are you there already?"

"Yeah. The roads weren't too bad, but they're getting worse by the minute. If you don't have to go out, I'd say you're better off staying home. They just announced on the radio that the police are advising people to do any traveling they have planned within the next hour. After that, they're going to ask everyone to stay put."

"Thanks for calling, Jack. I'll talk to you tomorrow."

Pat hung up the phone and turned to Gordon. "Jack says the police are telling people not to travel after the next hour."

"We better get that pizza ordered quickly, then. What do you feel like?"

"Tell you what. You order the pizza you would if you were home alone, and if I don't like it, I get to pick the next two pizzas we eat."

"It doesn't work with pizza," he joked.

"I think it does."

"Okay. I get to order any pizza I want?"

"Any pizza you want. I'll go open you a beer while you do that."

Gordon picked up the phone to start dialing when she interrupted him. "Oh, no anchovies."

"Okay."

Pat opened the fridge door and pulled out two beers. "Oh, let's not have anything really spicy either."

"Anything I want, hey?"

She poured his beer into a frosted mug and handed it to him. "Anything you want—just as long as it doesn't have any anchovies and it's not too spicy."

Gordon took the mug from her. "Anything else, before we're snowed in, woman?"

Pat laughed. "If there is, I'll let you know."

By 6:30, the movie was in the DVD player, and they had placed the pizza on the coffee table in front of the couch with plates and napkins. They were both still on their first beer, but Gordon had placed one more each on the table. "So we won't have to stop the movie," he had explained.

Pat had just pushed the play button when Gordon suddenly remembered something.

"Oh, just a minute. Don't start yet. I'll be right back."

A moment later he returned with a box of tissues. "So we won't have to stop the movie," he said again.

Pat was about to say something smart but knew she'd need the tissues and changed her mind. Mind you, she thought, I have used napkins before.

During the entire movie, Pat never said a word. Gordon had made a few comments in the beginning, but when he realized he wasn't going to get a reply, he stopped. At best, she would nod in response. He seemed to understand he had lost her to the emotions of the movie. When the movie was over, he looked at the three used tissues on the table.

"Wow. That was a three-tissue movie. Pretty good."

A little embarrassed, Pat chuckled. "I know," she said. "Some movies get to me every time, no matter how often I see them. This is one of them."

She stood up to clean the table and was surprised when he stood, took the plates from her hands, and placed them back on the table. She stood speechless as he reached over, put his arms around her, and held her close. "You fit so well. It's like you were made for me."

Pulling her down to the couch, arm still around her and keeping her close, he asked, "Do you believe in the perfect love?"

"Nothing's perfect, except love—even with all its imperfections."

"Do you believe everyone has a soul mate?"

This movie really got to him, she thought. She knew he was sensitive and caring, and they'd had some deep discussions, but never like this. Wondering where he was going with his questions, she answered, "Yes."

"There's something I want to talk to you about," he said, still holding her next to him.

"Okay," she said cautiously. She wasn't sure what was coming next, but for some reason, she was nervous.

He seemed to hesitate and then sat up, turned, and faced her. "Pat, I never really thought that a love existed where the happiness of the other person was all that really mattered. If I make you half as happy as you make me, well, then you've got to be the second happiest person in the world.

"Since I met you, I have fallen so deeply in love with you. I've seen you work, I've seen you laugh, I've seen you discipline, love, and play with your children, even when you were tired." He reached out and brushed her cheeks. "And I've seen you cry." He leaned over and kissed a dry tear on her cheek.

He sat back with a small grin on his face. "I've seen the look on your face when I do something that you don't particularly approve of . . . but I try not to see that one too often," he added.

Gordon took her hands in his, brought them to his lips, and kissed them. "I had planned this to be special. We were going to go out, and I was going to wine you and dine you with fine food, at one of the finest restaurants in town, instead of beer and pizza on the couch, but I don't want to wait any longer."

He slowly got off the couch and bent down on one knee. "Pat, I love you more than I could have ever imagined loving anyone. I love your kids and promise to treat them like they were my own, if you'll let me."

He reached into his pocket and pulled out a small box. Opening it and turning it towards her, he asked, "Will you marry me?"

Pat looked at the diamond ring glittering in front of her. This was totally a surprise to her. She thought they might be headed down this way but didn't expect it to happen for at least another year. She also had no doubts that she loved him and couldn't imagine life without him.

"I know we've only known each other since the summer," he continued, "but I have no doubt in my mind that I want to be with you for all the rest of my summers—and winters, falls, and springs. If you aren't sure, I understand and I'll wait until you are, but if you're as sure about us as I am, then I'd like to be your husband and spend the rest of my life doing everything I can to make you, Chelsea, and Nathan happy."

A tear ran down Pat's cheek, and then more followed. Unable to speak, she simply nodded until she could get out her reply. "Yes."

Gordon got up from the floor and sat next to her, grabbing her and holding her just as hard as he could. Pat laughed and cried while holding on just as tight.

"I love you so much. Thank God I found you," he said. Then he leaned down and kissed her, tasting the salt of her tears.

⁓ ⁓ ⁓ ⁓ ⁓ ⁓ ⁓ ⁓ ⁓ ⁓ ⁓ ⁓ ⁓ ⁓ ⁓ ⁓ ⁓ ⁓ ⁓

Nina snuggled more deeply into the blanket wrapped around her, trying to keep warm. The blizzard that had started hours ago was not letting up. The howling of the wind outside was all around and it haunted her. It was a lonely sound, one that did nothing to help Nina's depression.

With the blanket still wrapped around her, she went to the thermostat to read the temperature. Even though it read 23 degrees, she didn't believe it. She sat on the hearth of the fireplace hoping the heat of the fire would warm her.

Mark and Jan had been gone five days, and Nina's depression had only deepened. She had not answered the door or the telephone since they had left. She had made a point of returning Jan's call on Wednesday, but that was three days ago, and she had spoken to no one since.

Feeling a restlessness building inside her, Nina wandered the house. She realized, as she had a hundred times before, that every room was empty of any life until she entered it. When she left the room, she brought the emptiness of the room within her. There was no one here but her. It was the way of life for her now. It was an observation she had made many times before, but today the realities of it all seemed to shout out to her, "You are alone, and you will remain alone forever."

Was this all she had left to look forward to? Except for the occasional phone call, or the occasional visit, was she to be alone the rest of her life—every day, every hour, and every minute? She continued to roam the house with no one to talk to but the ghosts that would haunt her memories forever.

She entered the kitchen, opened the cupboard that held the liquor, and took out the bottle of scotch. It was rare that she poured a glass of wine now—it didn't have the effect she needed quickly enough. She poured the golden liquid into a glass and put the bottle on the counter—she didn't bother putting it away. She didn't try to kid herself anymore; she knew she'd be back for more.

Pulling back the drapes, she looked out the living room window. The blizzard made it impossible to see the houses across the street. The snow continued to come down, and the wind was not letting up. Nina felt as though she were the last living person on earth. God, she had never felt so alone.

She allowed the tears to fall as she held the glass to her lips and took a drink. She felt the liquid warm her when she swallowed. There was no need to control her pain or fears. There was no one to impress with her pretense of strength. There was no reason to look forward to tomorrow. It would just be another day like today, with a vacuum of emptiness that wrapped itself around her like the blanket she held close to her now. All she had now were her yesterdays.

Just as she was about to turn away, she thought she saw movement. Taking a second look, even in the darkness that the early evening brought this time of year, she was sure she spotted Matt standing by her front step. Leaning closer to the window to get a better look, she searched the front step and then followed the sidewalk as far as the blowing snow of the blizzard would allow her to see, but there was nothing—no Matt, and no footprints to indicate that anyone had been there. There was nothing but the snow piling up against the wall of the house.

My mind must be starting to play tricks on me, she thought. Why would anyone in his or her right mind be standing outside in this blizzard? Looking at her empty glass, she turned to go to the kitchen. At least this was one problem she could solve. The solution to her empty glass was sitting on her kitchen counter, just waiting for her.

She didn't bother with ice this time; the ice from the last drink had not had enough time to melt. She picked the bottle up and filled her glass. It wasn't until she was putting the bottle back on the counter that she noticed something sticking out from behind the canister. She put the bottle down and pulled the paper out from its hiding spot.

She could feel her heart pounding as she looked at the picture. It was a picture of her and Mike, arm in arm and standing by their motor home, which was parked in the front of their house. They had it taken just minutes before they left on their trip last summer. Without thinking, she placed her glass on the counter to free her hand. With one hand she held the picture; with the other she gently caressed Mike's face.

A tear fell and dropped on her hand holding the picture. Then another. She began to cry silent tears that soon turned to sobs as she collapsed on the kitchen floor. She held the picture so tight that it became bent and crumpled. The sobs soon turned to cries of despair—the same cries of a wounded animal that cried out, the sound piercing through the woods. Life would not allow her to die, and the pain would not allow her to live.

"God!" she shouted. "What have You done? Why did You take him? I was always told that You were the perfect God that knew everything. The almighty God that made no mistakes!"

Nina looked up and shook her fist. "Are You listening, God? Have You ever listened? Where were You when I was in the hospital asking You to save him? I asked You not to take him! You weren't listening then, were You? You made a mistake, God, didn't You? Admit it! You, the almighty God—the perfect God—You made a mistake."

Nina lowered her fist and tried to focus on the picture, but her tears blurred her vision. "If it wasn't a mistake, then You just don't care! We're just Your little play things, aren't we?"

She leaned back against the wall and sobbed. "I can't take it anymore! Do you hear me, God?" she cried. "I can't take it anymore."

She buried her head in her hands and shook as her tears dropped to the floor. Anger suddenly turned to defeat. "Oh, God," she quietly prayed. "What am I going to do? I don't know that I can go on."

Without knowing where she was going or what she was doing, she slowly stood. Maybe she didn't have to go on like this anymore. She remembered the pills in her medicine cabinet. It was suddenly so clear. The pain could be over.

As if in a fog, she methodically went through each room. Anything that was out of order was put into place. Making sure the last room was the en suite off her bedroom, she wiped the counter and sink, tidied the basket that held her makeup, and opened the medicine cabinet. There she found the prescription pills her doctor had given her. She brought them to the kitchen, placed them on the table, and went to retrieve her drink, along with the picture of her and Mike.

First she straightened out the picture as best she could and stood it up, leaning it against the empty bowl that was once always full of fruit. Next she took a sip from her glass, looking at the picture the entire time. She opened the prescription bottle, spilled the pills onto the table, and counted them; there were 14 left. Leaning back in her chair, she took another sip and reflected on the picture. She would need to explain to Mike why she had to do what she was doing.

"Mike, I'm so sorry. I can't do it. I just can't take it anymore. You were always the strong one, the one I leaned on. I'm no good without you."

Tears fell and she looked away. It was too difficult to look him in the eye, even if it was a crumpled picture. It was only the pictures and her memories of him that she had left. She knew that if he were here now, he would scold her. She was embarrassed by her weakness.

She defended her actions. "What do you expect me to do? I hardly remember a life without you. You were my everything, Mike—my strength, my joy, my very being. Without you, there is no me."

Nina picked up her glass and took a big swallow. She had no time to sip from the glass anymore.

"Please, Mike, try to understand, and when I cross over, please be there waiting to welcome me with open arms."

Nina placed the pills in a perfect line in front of her and studied them. Two glasses of scotch and 14 pills. Is that enough, she wondered? Better be sure. The only thing worse than what she was feeling now would be to wake up in the morning to find out she had failed. Nina emptied the contents of her glass down her throat. Wiping the spilled liquid from her chin with the sleeve of her sweatshirt, she poured herself a third drink. Anxious to complete her mission, she calculated that three glasses of scotch and 14 pills had a better chance of success. Failure was not an option.

Nina studied the tools of her scheme. There was one thing missing. Feeling the effects of the scotch, she began speaking to herself out loud. "Even a man who is about to be executed by being shot got a last cigarette," she reasoned. She lit a cigarette, placed it in the ashtray, and reached for the first sleeping pill when she heard a knocking. Jumping from the shock of the sudden noise, she listened closely. Except for the howling of the wind outside, there was only silence. Convincing herself that it had only been her imagination, or the wind outside, she was about to return to the task at hand when the doorbell rang.

Who in their right mind would be out tonight? The roads were closed, and the blowing snow made it so that a person would get lost even walking in their own neighbourhood. She sat, silently hoping that whoever it was would go away. After what seemed like an eternity, Nina decided that the person had left.

Once again, she reached out to pick up the first pill. She had the event planned out. She would take all 14 pills, one by one, and wash each down with a drink of scotch. When the pills were gone, she would have one more scotch and cigarette, then lie down on her bed and wait until she could see Mike again. With every drink from her glass, the plan made more sense. Starting her third glass of scotch, it now seemed like a plan without a flaw. Once again, just as she was about to pick up that first pill, she heard someone at the front door. The banging on the door nearly made her jump off her seat.

"Nina!" She faintly heard her name called. Then quietly and clearly, as if the person was standing right beside her, she heard, "Nina, answer the door. I can't come in unless you allow it."

Nina looked around, expecting to see someone standing beside her. There was nobody there; she was alone. Again, she heard, "Nina, answer the door. I can't come in unless you allow it."

Slowly, hesitantly, she stood. What was happening? She looked back at the table and silently counted the pills. All 14 were still there. Yes, this was her third glass of scotch, but that was not enough to start her hallucinating.

"Nina, let me in."

Standing motionless in front of the door now, she stared at it, uncertain of what to do. Was she finally, truly losing her mind?

"Open the door, Nina. I'm here to help."

Nina turned the handle and opened the door. There in front of her, stood Matt.

"May I come in?" he asked.

Nina opened the door wider and stood back. She was aware of the fact that she never felt the cold from the outside coming through the open doorway. As if in a trance, she stood silent as Matt entered her home, removed the door handle from her grasp, and closed the door.

"Thank you for allowing me in your home, Nina. Why don't we sit down?"

Nina simply nodded as Matt led the way to her kitchen. "If I recall," he said, "Mike used to make you a cup of tea when you were upset."

"How do you know what Mike did?" she quietly asked, puzzled by the entire incident.

"There's a lot I know, Nina, but we'll get to that later. First, let me make the tea, and then we'll talk."

Nina watched as he worked in the kitchen. He seemed to know where everything was without asking. How could this be? she wondered. He had been to her home a couple of times, but not often enough, and never had he helped out in the kitchen.

She knew that the events that were taking place in her home should upset her, and normally they would. Here was a man she barely knew showing up in the middle of a storm, talking about Mike as if they had known each other for years although they had never met, and he seemed to know his way around her kitchen as if it were his own. Yet Nina was surprised that she felt perfectly calm about the situation, just like every other time Matt was around her.

"Should I be afraid?" she asked.

"Not at all."

"Why are you here?"

"You asked for help," he said simply.

"I didn't ask you for help."

"I didn't say you asked me for help. I only said you asked for help. Now, the tea is ready. Why don't you sit down here, where you were," he said, as he guided her to the chair she had been sitting in.

Nina sat. How did he know where she had been sitting? It must be because the chair was pulled away from the table more than the others were, or he remembered where she had sat the last time that he was there.

Remembering what she was planning to do just before he arrived, Nina became embarrassed and worried that he might see the pills and scotch. She didn't want him to guess what she had been about to do and hoped that she could remove any evidence before he noticed. She reached out to where she had left them, but they were gone. Confused, she looked around. Had she bumped them when she got up to answer the door? They were nowhere in sight. Feeling rather foolish and confused, she leaned over to check under the table.

"The scotch and pills have been put away," he said, knowing exactly what she was looking for. Nina sat up and stared at him in silence and in disbelief. What was going on? Nina stood abruptly. She knew she hadn't put them away, and Matt hadn't left her sight since arriving. Feeling like she was losing her mind, she decided go to the medicine cabinet and look for herself.

"You can check if you want, but I'm telling you, they have been put away."

"What do you mean?" she asked.

"The pills. That's what you're going to look for, isn't it? They are back in the medicine cabinet. If you want to check you can, but I would prefer they stay where they are for now, if you don't mind."

Nina never spoke a word. She simply left the room to look in the medicine cabinet for herself. She didn't see them at first, because they weren't in the same place she normally kept them. She always kept them on the bottom shelf, front and centre. It wasn't until she was about to close the cabinet door that she spotted them. They were on the top shelf, behind her small container of cotton swabs.

Back in the kitchen, Matt was waiting for her. "I told you they were put away, didn't I? I don't have the ability to throw them away, Nina. Only you can do that."

He guided her back to the table, and they each took a seat.

"Your tea is getting cold. You should drink it."

Obediently, Nina drank her tea. Silence filled the air as Nina tried to make sense of it all, but there didn't seem to be any sense to be made of it. When the tea was drunk, Nina was surprised that any effects she'd had from the alcohol were gone.

"Why are you here?" she asked.

"You asked for help"

"But, I didn't ask you for help," she repeated herself from when he first entered her kitchen.

"Not me. God. You asked God for help, and He sent me."

"I asked God for help many times. Why didn't He help me then? Why didn't He help me when I asked Him to help Mike in the hospital? Why did He wait until now?"

"God has helped you. In fact, he blessed you with a miracle before you even asked Him."

"Yeah, my life is full of miracles," she responded bitterly.

"Sometimes God will perform a miracle, and you won't even know it."

"I can't believe that God has performed any miracles for me."

"That's because you humans think that the only time God performs a miracle is when you get what you ask for."

Nina carried her cup to the sink, rinsed it out, and put it on the counter. Turning to face Matt, she leaned against the counter and crossed her arms.

"Well, you are right about one thing. If God has performed a miracle, I don't know it."

Matt sat in silence, waiting until she was ready to hear the rest. Slowly, she sat back down at the table and looked at him.

"What do you mean when you say God sent you? And why did you say 'you humans,' like you're not one yourself? What are you then, an angel?"

"God heard your cry for help. He has been with you all your life, Nina. He was with you the day you brought Mike to the hospital, and He has been with you all these months. That's why He sent me to watch over you, but you weren't ready for me, so I just watched and waited until you were ready."

"If God has been with me, then why did He take Mike? He was a good man with a good heart. Why did God take him?"

"God didn't take him, Nina. Mike's death was of his own doing."

"Don't you say that!" she lashed out. "Mike didn't want to die. Mike never wanted to die, and he never wanted to leave me!"

"You're right, Mike didn't want to leave you, but his death was his own doing."

"I don't want to talk to you anymore. Go away!"

"Are you sure?"

"You said you came because I asked for help. Well, now I'm asking you to leave, so you should. Go away," she repeated.

"Are you saying you don't want help anymore?"

"I don't like the way you help."

"I didn't ask that, Nina. I want to know if you're telling God you don't want help anymore."

Nina knew she couldn't carry on the way she had been. A tear escaped as she shook her head. "No," she whispered.

"Nina, you know that Mike had been warned about his smoking and the stress level in his business life. You know he had been due for another check-up four months before he died, but he kept putting it off. Is your definition of God's help or a miracle to take away all consequences of a person's behaviour?"

"Yes. No," she stammered. "There was no warning. He should have given a warning."

"Mike knew he wasn't feeling right, but he still kept putting off going to the doctor. Would it have made a difference if you had known? Would it have made you grieve any less?"

"No, but Mike was a good man. He shouldn't have died. It was the wrong time. We just got to the point in our lives where we could slow down and enjoy life more."

"At what point is the right time, Nina? Ten years ago, when you still had children at home? Five years from now, when he was ready to retire?"

"You don't understand," she said simply.

"I do understand; it's you who doesn't. You are right, Nina. Mike was a good man. You also are a good person, and that is why God performed the miracle He did."

"Why do you keep talking about this miracle that God performed? This is not a miracle."

"Nina, God performs miracles all the time, but He doesn't announce them. He is not such a vain God that He needs to make every miracle He performs known to man. He performs these miracles out of love for His children. When you do something for your children, do you do it for their gratitude, or for the love you have for them?

"Mike had already established his death. On the other hand, without God stepping in, there would have been some very different consequences. Without God stepping in, the consequences would have affected many lives. The miracle He blessed you with was because of His love."

"What do you mean?"

"Maybe we should talk more after you've slept. You look awfully tired, Nina. Why don't you lie down, and we'll talk more when you wake up?"

Nina, who had been wide awake just moments before, realized now just how tired she had suddenly become. She could hardly keep her eyes open. It must have been from the scotch, she reasoned, knowing full well that she had not felt the effects of the alcohol since Matt had entered her home.

"I don't understand how this came on so suddenly," she said with a yawn. "Maybe you're right. I'll just take a little nap."

"You go get into bed. If you need me, I'll be here. As long as you need me, I won't leave," he said as Nina stood. "Always remember that even in our darkest hours, when we feel most alone, we are not. Someone is always looking over you."

Not understanding why it didn't feel strange for her to go to bed while a man she had not known very long sat in her kitchen, Nina quietly and calmly made her way to the bedroom.

Slowly, Nina got under the covers. As she lay her head down, her thoughts were on the man in her kitchen. In her heart, she knew he was like no other man she had ever met. What did he mean when he said "On the other hand, without God stepping in, there would have been some very different consequences"? She had a lot more questions she needed answered, but right now, more than anything she needed sleep.

Sunday, August 12

NINA SLOWLY STRETCHED IN AN attempt to bring herself out of a deep sleep and into what could at least be considered semiconsciousness. As she reached out to the other side of the bed, she realized that Mike was already up. The realization at first did not surprise her. He had always been an early riser.

Abruptly she sat up as panic set in. Where was he? Something was wrong, but she couldn't remember what. What was it?

"Mike!" she called his name with terror in her voice. "Mike, where are you?"

Throwing the blankets back, she continued to call for him. "Mike!" She had to find him. Something was terribly wrong. What was it that she couldn't remember?

Screaming his name, she jumped out of bed and bolted for the bedroom door to find him just as he came running in. He had been fixing their breakfast when he heard her call his name. The panic in her voice had apparently registered with him, because he ran down the hall to find her

"Nina, what's wrong?"

The sight of him took her breath away. Speechless, she froze as she took in the very sight of him, not completely sure she should trust what she was seeing.

"Nina," he repeated, "what's wrong?"

Throwing her arms around him, she held him as close to her as she possibly could. Suddenly and without warning, the tears came, followed by sobs.

Mike picked her up, walked over to the bed, and sat down. He held her tightly on his lap without saying a word. He seemed to know that there was no point in asking her what was wrong until she had control of her emotions. It was a few minutes before the sobbing subsided. He reached for a tissue from her nightstand and wiped her tears.

"What's wrong, Honey? What got you so upset?"

"I . . . I don't know," she said, shaking her head. "When I woke up and you weren't there, I thought something was wrong. For some reason . . ." She stopped and looked at him, gently caressing his cheek. "I thought something had happened to you. I thought I had lost you," she quietly said.

Mike wiped away her tears. "Nothing has happened. I'm right here."

"I . . . I thought I'd never see you again," she said, still trying to get control.

"No such luck," he said, trying to calm her down by making light of it. He could feel her body shaking.

"Mike, don't joke about it. I don't know what I would do if you weren't here." The tears began again, followed by soft sobs as she snuggled into his shoulder.

Mike continued to hold her tight, rocking her back and forth until he felt her begin to relax in his arms. When she had settled down, he leaned back and held her chin, raising it up so that she was looking at him.

"You know what I think happened," he said. "I think you had a bad dream, that's all. I'm here and I'm fine. I've got breakfast started and coffee on. Why don't you take a shower, and when you're done, breakfast will be waiting for you."

Nina nodded. "Okay." Mike put her on the bed next to him, gave her a kiss on the forehead, and stood up.

"Mike," she called as he was leaving the room. He stopped and turned. "I love you," was all she said.

"I love you too, Nina, and don't worry. If I have any say in the matter, I'll be here for a long time."

Nina stepped into their en suite and looked at her reflection in the bathroom mirror. She had been so tired the night before that she had contemplated going straight to bed without taking her makeup off. She was grateful now that she had thought better of it and removed the makeup, otherwise she would have raccoon eyes from all the crying. As it was, she couldn't get over how terrible she looked. Between the late night and the early morning cry, the bags under her eyes aged her by 10 years in a matter of just 12 hours.

Maybe Mike was right. Maybe it was just a bad dream. What else could it be? Everything was fine when they went to bed last night, and they hadn't spoken with anyone since. Again she asked herself what else it could be, and she still couldn't come up with a better explanation than a bad dream, just like Mike said.

Surely once she showered and had breakfast, she would feel better, she reasoned. Nina swallowed a couple of Tylenol and stepped into the shower. Standing under the spray of water, Nina tried to wash away her uneasy feeling. If it was a bad dream, she couldn't remember it. Never could she remember a dream having an effect on her the way this one did—if it was a dream. Somehow, she couldn't help feeling that there was something more to it.

By the time Nina made her way to the kitchen, showered, dressed, and ready for the day, the table was set and Mike was putting their plates of bacon, eggs, diced potatoes, and sliced tomatoes on the table. He looked up as she entered, apparently pleased that she was calmer than she had been twenty minutes earlier.

"Good timing," he said. "Breakfast, as promised."

They each sat at their places at the table, and she noticed Mike studying her as she laid the napkin on her lap. She knew that he wanted to ask her if she was feeling better but must have thought better of it. She was sure that whatever it was that had upset her earlier even scared him. Over the years he had seen her get upset, but she had never been like she was less than an hour before. And the most baffling thing of it all was that there didn't appear to be a reason.

After breakfast was eaten, Mike went out to clean the patio table and chairs of any dust that may have blown on them, and Nina cleared the kitchen table and poured coffee. Joining him on the deck, she sat back and closed her eyes for a moment.

"That's a warm sun already," she said.

"The weatherman has promised that it will be 32°C by midafternoon. It might be a good idea to get as much work done out here as we can, before it gets too hot."

Nina lit a cigarette and studied him through the smoke. She knew that Mike was aware that she was observing him just as she had throughout breakfast. She wondered if he would bring up the subject of what it was that had upset her so. If he even considered it, he must have decided against it, because the subject was not brought up by either.

Holding the cigarette up as if inspecting it, Nina looked from the cigarette to her husband. "Do you think we should quit?"

"What?"

"Do you think we should quit?" she repeated. "Quit smoking, I mean."

"No. We've tried before but haven't been able to. What makes you think this time would be any different? Besides," he continued, "I enjoy it and I've come to terms that I am addicted, but I don't care. Let the rest of the world quit if they want to. I, for one, have decided to quit quitting."

"We know they're bad for us, though. Maybe we should just think about it."

"I *have* thought about it, and like I said, I've made up my mind. Nina, I don't want to talk about this anymore. Don't let that stop you from quitting, though." Then he must have realized that she was still feeling the aftermath of her earlier anxiety, and he immediately softened his voice.

"Sweetheart, I don't know what it is that upset you earlier, but I'm fine and I'm not going anywhere. We don't even know what it is that has you so scared. Please try to let it go."

Nina knew he was right. If she didn't let it go, neither one would have any peace.

The remainder of their coffees and cigarettes were in silence, each into their own thoughts. Nina wondered what she could say to make Mike take better care of himself.

Finally, Mike put his cigarette out in the ashtray and rose. "Well, I'd better get at it before it gets too hot."

Nina stood. "Mike, would you just hold me for a minute, please?"

Mike walked over and put his arms around her. "Anytime," he said as he kissed the top of her head.

They stood like that on the deck for a few minutes before Mike took a step back and looked at her. "I don't want you to worry. My father lived until he was in his eighties and I feel fine. Promise me you won't worry, it was just a dream."

"Was it, Mike? I don't even remember dreaming. What if it was a premonition?"

Mike heard the quiver in her voice and knew she was doing the best she could to control her emotions. "You may not be able to remember it, but your subconscious does, that's all. I don't believe in premonitions. What I like about today and everyday is the fact that I don't know what will happen. Each day has its own possibilities. It's what keeps life interesting."

Mike cupped her face in his hands and looked into her eyes, trying to convince her that he would be all right. Then he repeated himself, "Nina, promise me you won't worry."

Nina saw the concern in his eyes and heard it in his voice. He had always been there for her, and she didn't want him to worry about her. "I promise I'll try," she said for his benefit. She turned and went into the house to finish cleaning up.

With the last dish washed and placed on the draining board, Nina wiped her hands on the tea towel. Normally she dried the dishes and put them away before leaving the kitchen, but today, before finishing up, she decided to go to the deck and reassure herself that Mike was indeed working in the backyard, alive and well.

As soon as she spotted him, she felt foolish for letting the bad dream upset her so. By now, she had convinced herself that he was right; it was just a bad dream, and she had to try to quit thinking about it. Just as she was about to go back into the house to finish dishes, he spotted her.

"Hey, Babe," he said, "Done dishes already?"

Embarrassed at being caught, she decided not to tell him that the real reason she was there was to check on him. "Not quite, but if it's going to get as hot as you said, I thought you should be careful not to get dehydrated, and I wondered if you needed anything to drink."

"Actually, that's a good idea. If you bring me a glass, I'll drink water from the tap out here."

"Your wish is my command," she said, proud of herself for her quick thinking to cover up her real reason for being there.

That evening Nina made a gourmet salad while Mike barbequed the steaks. She realized now how foolish she had been to get so upset about something that hadn't even happened. Not only had it not happened, but she had no reason to believe it even *would* happen. She was bound and determined to make up for the worry she had caused Mike.

The day had been spent in quiet companionship, working side by side, and by the end of the day, the leaves had been raked, the lawn had been mowed, and the fence had been stained. Mike cleaned the brushes and put them away, along with the trays and any leftover stain, and Nina went in to shower. Later, while Mike showered, she carefully styled her hair, applied makeup, and put on a clean outfit.

She purposely chose the white shorts that she wouldn't have dared wear in public. She considered them much too short for a woman her age, but Mike liked them on her. Today no one else would see her in them but him.

He often told her that she still had the body she had when she was young, and when she wore those shorts, it made him feel twenty all over again. She knew what her body was like when she was twenty and she knew what her body looked like now. She also knew that the two were not even close to being the same. But when he said it, she also felt twenty all over again.

Next, she chose a red tank top that showed off the rest of her body. It really wasn't too revealing, but the way it clung to her body certainly left little to the imagination—and that was the result she was hoping for tonight. After twenty eight years of marriage, Nina was pleased that the physical attraction between her and Mike was still strong.

With the table set, she closed all the blinds to keep any sunlight out and lit the candles that had been placed next to the freshly cut flowers. Stepping back, she inspected the table. Perfection, she thought.

An hour later, Nina placed her empty wineglass next to her dinner plate. Everything had turned out exquisite, in Nina's opinion. It had been a dinner fit for a five-star restaurant.

"Cleanup is pretty easy," she said. "Why don't you cover the barbeque while I put the coffee on and load the dishwasher?"

"You're on," Mike said, as he stood to leave.

Nina had just loaded the dishwasher and was reaching for two liqueur glasses for the Grand Marnier she planned to serve with the coffee when she felt Mike come up behind her, wrapping his arms around her and kissing her neck.

"Do you have any idea how sexy you are in that outfit?" he asked.

"I was hoping you would think so."

He turned her around and brushed her lips with his own, teasing her with silent promises of more. He made good on his promise and kissed her deeply but gently, letting his tongue explore her mouth. His hands moved down her back and then back up the front, stopping to fondle her breasts. Nina's arms went around his neck as she returned his passion. He pressed himself against her, letting her feel the effect she was having on him.

"Come here," he said, "I have a surprise for you." His voice was hoarse from passion as he took her hand and led her from the kitchen.

Nina followed, feeling the weakness in her knees. As he led her into the living room, she saw that in front of the fireplace, he had placed their sheepskin rug and two more glasses of wine. He sat her down on the sheepskin rug and then sat down facing her, wrapping his legs around her. He reached over for the wineglasses, handed her one and clinked her glass with his own, and made a toast.

"To my wife, the best wife any man could ask for. I'm as much in love with you today as I was the day we married."

They each had a sip before he took the glass from her hand and placed it on the hearth of the fireplace, along with his own.

"Do you know, we haven't made love in front of the fireplace since before Mark was born," he said.

Nina giggled. "If I recall," she said, "that was about nine months before Mark was born."

Mike laughed, kissed her, and then gently lay her down on the rug.

Friday, August 17

NINA STOOD ON THE FRONT step and kissed her husband good-bye as he left for work. Her emotions from Sunday had subsided to concern by Monday and an uneasiness by Wednesday. Now, five days later, an appreciation of what she had in her life had settled in with only fleeting moments of edginess.

Last night, after supper, Nina and Mike drank their evening coffees on the deck, as they did whenever the weather allowed. It was then that he confided in her that he thought maybe it was time that they thought of semiretirement. He didn't think their finances would allow a full retirement, but he wasn't ready for that yet, anyway. They already had an appointment to meet with their financial planner on Saturday, so they decided to run the idea past her at that time to see if she thought they were financially able.

Shortly after Mike left, Nina was pulling weeds from her flower garden, and images of the two of them on an extended camping trip, or travels to Europe, or the Caribbean filled her thoughts. She really was lucky, she decided, and she was glad that she actually appreciated what she had and didn't just take it for granted.

By ten o'clock, the sun was getting warm. Nina had gone inside to get herself a glass of water and a hat when the phone rang. For some reason, the phone made her jump, and she thought twice about answering it.

Don't be stupid, she told herself. This is not woman's intuition, but just dumb, plain worrying about nothing. Mike was right. It had been nothing more than a dream that, for some reason, she just couldn't remember. She only wished she could remove the effects of the dream the same way that she had removed the memory of it. It wasn't until she answered the phone and heard Pat McDermott's voice that she actually relaxed.

"Pat, we were just talking about you last night."

"Good things only, I hope."

"Always," Nina responded with a smile.

Both she and Mike liked Pat and enjoyed working with her, which is why they referred her to anyone finding themselves in need of a financial planner.

"Good. I'm just phoning to confirm our appointment for tomorrow. Are we still on?"

"We are, indeed. In fact, that's what Mike and I were talking about. I don't know if you need to know ahead of time, but we want to talk to you about starting our retirement early."

"I haven't reviewed your file yet, but if memory serves me right, weren't you going to wait a couple more years?"

"Oh, I know—and I don't mean a full retirement. Mike was going to find out about contracting himself to the company. That way, he wouldn't work full time. These days, with computers, faxes, and phones, he may not even have to be in the office when he is working. Not all the time, anyway. He thinks that if our finances will allow it, the semiretirement will help him ease into the full retirement. He's concerned about going from having a hectic life one day to having nothing to do the next."

"Tell you what," Pat said, "you and Mike think about what it is you have in mind, and I'll review your file. Tomorrow, we'll see what we can come up with."

After Nina hung up the phone, she smiled to herself. Life was good.

That night after supper, Nina repeated her conversation with Pat to Mike.

"That reminds me," he said, going to the front closet. Nina saw him reach into his coat pocket and come back with a small box. When he handed it to her, she saw that is had been meticulously wrapped in blue paper, with a small white bow on top to finish it off. As much as Mike was a perfectionist, Nina knew that when it came to wrapping, he was all thumbs. It was obvious to her that he had not wrapped this gift.

"What's this?" she asked, taking the gift from him.

"Well, if I was just going to tell you, I wouldn't have gone to all the trouble of making that poor clerk at the store wrap it, would I? Open it and find out."

Laughing at the fact that Mike had just confirmed her suspicions, she ripped the paper off. She had never been one to slowly and deliberately unwrap any gift so that the paper could be saved; she felt that every new gift deserved new wrapping paper.

When the box was opened and the contents revealed, her hand reached out to caress a beautiful necklace. At the end of the chain was a pendant in the shape of a globe. She stood speechless as Mike reached over and took the box from her hand.

"Turn around," he said. "I want to see what it looks like on you."

"Wait," she said, taking the box back. "I want to look at a little longer."

"Do you know what it is?"

"Of course," she said. "It's a globe."

"It's my promise to you, that I will do everything I can so that we can have a good life from now on."

"Our life has already been pretty good up until now," she replied

"Oh, Sweetheart, I know that. I didn't mean to imply that we haven't. If I were to die tomorrow, I want to you to know that I died a happy man. We've been lucky. We've had a good marriage, where others we know haven't. A lot of people we know are divorced, or they're just plain miserable. We raised two great kids. I'm really very proud of them—and of us. We made it happen."

Mike took the necklace from her hand and turned her around so he could put it around her neck.

"I also know that we've made sacrifices, and while I don't begrudge them, we shouldn't have to make them anymore. I promise you that if it is within my power, from now on, there will be more time for us to be together, to travel, and to do all the things we've been talking about and planning for during these past few years. This globe represents the world, and I think it is time we start seeing more of it. What do you say we finally take that Caribbean cruise we've been talking about?"

He turned her back around to face him. "How does next March sound to you?"

Tears welled up in Nina's eyes. "Oh, Mike. Thank you," she said, caressing the necklace he had just placed around her neck.

As a tear fell down her cheek, she thought of what he had just promised her. "If it is within my power, from now on, there will be more time for us to be together." She had known this man a long time and had never known anything that was not within his power. If ever he decided it was to be, then it was so.

Saturday, August 18

"MIKE, HOW LONG ARE YOU going to work out there? Pat will be here in less than an hour."

"Then I have less than an hour to work."

Exasperated, Nina leaned against the railing of the deck. "Michael Vincent Andrews, are you not going to get yourself cleaned up before she gets here?"

"Well, to be honest with you, I wasn't planning on it," he replied, but they both knew that once she used his full name like that, he had very little chance of winning any discussion between them.

Mike pushed the end of the shovel into the dirt, leaned on it, and looked up at his wife, who stood three feet above him.

"This is not a social event, Nina, and I'm just going to get dirty again after she leaves. It's silly to take a shower, get all cleaned up, and then have to do it all over again later."

Nina hated to admit it, but what he said made sense. "Okay, tell you what. You work for another half-hour, and then you at least come in to wash your hands and face, and put some clean clothes on. Even if this isn't a social event, you don't have to be tracking dirt all over the house I just cleaned."

"Yes, Dear," he said, sounding as hen-pecked as he could.

"Don't be using that tone with me," she threw back at him, trying not to smile. She knew he was teasing her.

"Yes, Dear."

"Men," was all she said as she turned around and headed back into the house.

Just as she pulled the screen door back, she heard Mike call her. Stopping, she turned and faced him.

"I love you," he said, with his boyish smile.

She wasn't really mad, but she didn't mind him throwing in a little charm, just to be on the safe side. Her smile was her only reply.

Half an hour later, Mike was in their bedroom changing. When he came out, he poured a coffee from the freshly brewed pot, sat down, and pulled out a cigarette.

"Uh oh."

Nina had been putting buttercups and cupcakes on a small plate for their company; even if this wasn't a social event, there was nothing wrong with good manners. She stopped what she was doing and looked over to her husband.

"What's wrong?" she asked.

"I forgot to get cigarettes. This is my last one."

"Well, smoke mine."

"I don't like yours; they're so weak you can't even tell you're smoking. I'm going to run down to the store to get some more."

"There isn't time."

"There's plenty of time if we don't discuss it. The store isn't that far away. Besides, if she gets here before I get back, you can get her a coffee and feed her some of your tasty treats while she gets her papers out. I won't be long," he shouted as he shut the door behind him.

〃〃〃〃〃〃〃〃〃〃〃〃〃〃〃〃〃〃

Pat went through her briefcase one last time, making sure she didn't forget anything. Satisfied, she headed for the door.

"Okay, guys, I'm out of here."

Chelsea and Nathan came running to the door to see her off.

"I shouldn't be more than a couple of hours, and then we'll go to the mall and buy you both some new school clothes."

She hugged them both, said good-bye to Kelly, and was out the door. She hated that her job took her away from her children so much, but she also knew that it was her job that allowed them the lifestyle they had.

Pat looked at her wristwatch. She had 15 minutes to make the trip, which meant she wouldn't be late, but she didn't have any time to spare either. She put the car into reverse and backed out of the driveway, waved to Chelsea and Nathan, who were looking out the window of the house, and started on her way.

〃〃〃〃〃〃〃〃〃〃〃〃〃〃〃〃〃〃

Mike thought of Nina as he maneuvered the car through the traffic. If he had done his calculations correctly, Pat would confirm that a semiretirement at this point in their lives would be possible The more he thought about it, the more he thought that it probably was a better plan to ease into this, rather than going into full retirement right from the beginning.

The store was in sight now, just across the intersection at the bottom of the hill. If he was able to time it right, he would get a green light at the intersection, drive straight through, and turn left into the parking lot of the store. As he turned his neck to do a shoulder check for traffic, making sure it was safe to change lanes, he felt a sudden pain. The pain was so vicious it made him cry out. Mike's last thought before losing consciousness was that it was like a knife being plunged into his skull.

~~~~~~~~~~~~~~~~~~~

Pat glanced at her wristwatch, making sure she wasn't late. Three minutes to ten. With all things going her way, it would take two and a half minutes to get to the Andrews' house. She always prided herself on being a couple minutes early, but somehow the time had just got away from her this morning. She hated cutting it this close.

She turned her vision back to the road just in time to see the white car coming straight towards her. With reflex action, she turned the wheel, trying to swerve out of its way, but she was unsuccessful. Instead of a head-on-collision, the white car crashed into her driver's door. It was the impact of Pat's head against the glass that shattered the window. She died instantly.

The traffic came to a sudden halt. People who had been walking down the sidewalk stopped to stare. Time suddenly stood still.

"Did you see that?" they said to one another. "It's only ten o'clock in the morning, but I think that guy was drunk. He was driving like a maniac—swerved right into the other lane."

~~~~~~~~~~~~~~~~~~~

Nina looked out the living room window watching for Mike. Where was that man? It was a couple minutes after ten and, if he didn't hurry, Pat would be there before he returned. After checking once again that she had laid out any papers she thought they would need for the meeting, she glancing at her watch again and saw that it was now 10:15. He should have been back by now, and she was beginning to worry.

It wasn't until 10:30, after pacing the house several times, that she realized Pat had not yet arrived either. That was not like her; she had never been late for an appointment before, and she had phoned to confirm just yesterday, so Nina knew it was today. She must have got caught up at another appointment, Nina reasoned. She'd probably be phoning anytime now to say she was running behind. Nina was silently grateful that Pat hadn't arrived on time, only to find that Mike wasn't there.

Where is Mike? she wondered for the hundredth time. Nina contemplated going out to look for him but realized that that would mean there would be no one there to greet Pat when she did arrive.

Nina decided to phone the store instead. The two of them went there often enough that the clerks knew both her and Mike. Maybe they could tell her what time he had left the store. She had just pulled the phone book out to find their number when the doorbell rang.

Nina went to the door expecting to find Pat on the other side, but instead there was a policeman in full uniform.

"Mrs. Andrews?"

Nina hesitated. She knew instinctively that she did not want to be a part of the conversation that was about to take place. All colour drained from Nina's face. She had never heard of an officer delivering good news. From this moment on, her life would never be the same.

"Yes," she whispered.

"I'm afraid there has been an accident."

Nina's chin began to quiver, and she fought the impulse to close the door.

"May I come in?" he asked.

Nina barely moved back to give him room to step through the doorway. The officer had to turn sideways to get through the small opening she made for him. He took the door handle from her and closed the door behind him. Nina seemed frozen to her spot.

"Mrs. Andrews, there has been an accident that involved a Michael Andrews. We have this as being his address. Is that correct?"

Nina nodded again.

The officer hesitated. Nina just stood motionless and speechless, staring, waiting for him to go on.

Finally he asked, "Is Michael Andrews your husband?"

Nina nodded once again. For some reason she was finding it impossible to speak.

"Mrs. Andrews, I'm sorry to have to tell you that your husband was killed in a car accident."

"*Nooo!*" she screamed, and then she said more softly, "No," backing away from him.

The officer took her arm and guided her to the couch. "Sit here. I'll get you some water," he said before making his way to find the kitchen. He came back with a glass half-full of water. "Here, drink this," he said, as he handed it to her.

She brought the glass to her mouth to do as she had been told, but she was shaking so badly that a few drops fell on her chin. None of the liquid reached her mouth. She put the glass on the table, unaware that she had placed it on the coaster without thinking.

"Mrs. Andrews, is there anyone I can call to come over—maybe one of your neighbours?"

Nina nodded.

"Who, Mrs. Andrews? You tell me who to call, and I will."

"I don't know who I should call. Our children live out of town. They have to know, don't they? How do I tell them? What do I tell them?"

"Mrs. Andrews," the officer said, "is there a neighbour or a friend close by that I can call for you?"

"Okay."

"Who would that be, Mrs. Andrews?"

"Scott and Carrie."

"Mrs. Andrews, who are Scott and Carrie?"

Thoughts started going through Nina's mind faster than she could keep up. *I knew something was going to happen. I told Mike to be careful. It wasn't just a dream.*

"Mrs. Andrews," the officer repeated. "Who are Scott and Carrie?"

Nina looked at him, trying to comprehend what was going on.

"Scott and Carrie? They're my neighbours. Why?"

"Do you want me to call them for you?"

"Okay."

"Where do they live?"

Nina sat perfectly still, pointing in the direction of their house.

"Do they live next door?"

"Yes."

He hurried out the door, apparently not wanting her to be alone for long. Within four minutes of leaving Nina on the couch, the officer returned with Scott and Carrie.

Carrie ran to the couch and sat next to Nina, putting her arms around her. Nina just sat there motionless, staring into space. She hadn't moved since the officer left to get her neighbours.

"Here, Nina, drink some of this," Carrie said, handing her the glass of water from the table. Nina did so dutifully.

In the meantime, the officer was explaining to Scott what had happened. "I have to ask her some questions."

"Now?" Scott questioned. "I don't know if she is capable of answering."

"There are just a couple of questions. The witnesses said he was driving erratically. There will be a blood sample for the alcohol content in his body, but I should ask her. Maybe she can help us determine what happened."

"Officer, I can assure you that Mike was not one to be drinking this early in the morning—and he would never drink and drive," Scott said. "Your blood sample will confirm that, so you don't need to ask her. If you have any questions later, I'll make sure she is available."

The officer looked over to Nina sitting on the couch and then left.

Sunday, August 19

JACK LAY IN THE BED he had once shared with Pat. Chelsea had finally fallen asleep on one side of him and Nathan on the other. It had been a long night, but light trickled in through the bedroom drapes now, letting him know that night had passed.

He looked at his children lying next to him and wondered, as he had a hundred times during the night, how were they going to get through this. He was their only parent now, and he didn't know if he was up to the task.

How would any of them get along without Pat? She was the essence of their lives, the centre of their unit. It was a defective unit, he admitted, but it was because of her that it still worked. She was the one who provided the strength, the warmth, and the discipline. All their lives were better because of her, and he couldn't even fathom what any of their lives were going to be like without her. Nathan and Chelsea still needed her to love them and to help mold them as they grew.

Jack knew he had dozed off a few times during the night, but he would have been surprised if all the minutes he slept added up to more than an hour. He decided to hire a taxi for the day. He didn't trust himself to be capable enough to handle a vehicle today, and the last thing that Chelsea and Nathan needed now was to lose another parent in an accident.

Lying in bed next to his children, Jack made a mental list of things that had to be done so that he could arrange for the burial of Chelsea and Nathan's mother. Over the next few days, he would make several trips to the lawyer and the bank. He would need to have full custody of the children acknowledged. He would have to give up his place and arrange to move back here. It would be too much change for Chelsea and Nathan to move from here. They didn't need any more changes in their lives.

Jack realized that he would have laughed aloud at the irony of it all, had it not hurt so badly. Their last argument before the breakup was because Jack listed the house without talking to Pat. He had decided they should move. In the end, he had moved—but he moved alone, leaving his family behind. Now, here he was moving back in, but without the only woman he had ever really loved. What a real jackass you are, Jack McDermott, he thought, just as the phone rang.

Jack reached for the phone to answer it as quickly as he could, so as not to wake his children. Quietly he said, "Hello?" as he left the bed with as little movement as possible, taking the cordless phone into the next room.

"Is Pat there?"

"Who's asking, please?"

"My name is Gordon Atkins. Who's this?"

"Gordon, this is Jack McDermott, Pat's husband."

"Oh . . ."

Jack noticed the pause on the other end of the line and guessed what this phone call was about. Had Pat been seeing this man? he wondered.

"Listen, I'm sorry for calling. I understood that Pat was no longer married. Obviously, I misunderstood."

Okay, they hadn't been seeing each other yet, but clearly Gordon was calling to change that.

"Gordon . . ." Jack said before the man on the other end of the line could hang up. Then he paused, wondering what to say next and why he felt the need to tell him anything.

Should he be vague and just let the guy figure it out for himself? *Pat's unavailable to take your call right now.* Or maybe he should let this guy know that he shouldn't wait for her to return his call. *Pat's not taking any calls right now—or ever again.* Or, how about just getting right to the point. *Sorry, buddy, you're too late.*

There was a long pause as Jack went over the different responses in his mind. The pause grew awkward, and it was Gordon who broke the silence. "I'm sorry . . ." he began, and Jack cut him off.

Jack felt his voice quiver, but he knew that what he was about to say would be repeated many times over the next few days. "No, Gordon, I'm sorry. There's no easy way to say this. Pat was killed in a car accident yesterday. I'm here taking care of our children."

"Oh . . . I am sorry."

"Thanks," was all Jack said, and he hung up.

Jack was in the kitchen now and proceeded to make coffee. There were a lot of phone calls to make, and it was probably best to make them while Chelsea and Nathan slept. He had thought of making them yesterday, but the children had needed him, and that had been his priority. By the time he got them settled, he was drained and needed time for himself. Then, it was too late to call anyone. There was nothing anyone could do at two in the morning, except lose sleep.

The first person he needed to call was Nancy. Not only should she know, but also she could help by contacting clients who had upcoming appointments. They would need to be told.

Jack knew Nancy was going to take it hard, but then who wasn't? Everyone who knew Pat would feel a void in their lives. Jack went over in his mind what he should tell Nancy? He knew she lived alone. At first he thought of asking her to come over to the house before breaking it to her, but he quickly discarded that idea. He knew it wouldn't help Chelsea or Nathan to see her upset. Besides, he didn't know if he had any more strength in him right now to be her shoulder.

Should he call someone else to go to her apartment so she wasn't alone? In the end, he decided just to call her. Somehow she would have to handle it, just like everyone else would have to. Jack got himself a cup from the cupboard, filled it with coffee, and took a swallow. Putting it on the counter, he picked up the phone and dialed. She answered on the third ring.

"Hello, Nancy," he started. "It's Jack. I've got some bad news."

Monday, August 20

MARK OPENED THE DOOR, AND before he could close it behind him, Jan was running up to greet him.

"We have to be quiet," she whispered. "Mom took one of the pills we got from the doctor for her, and I think she's finally getting some sleep."

"How is she?" Mark asked his sister.

"About the same. I don't know what to do. I want to ask questions about the arrangements, but I'm afraid it will upset her. She's getting lots of calls, but she's not taking any of them, and she still hasn't had anything to eat."

"Well, at least she's getting some sleep now."

Mark looked at his sister with concern. "How are you doing?"

"Okay . . . you know . . . I don't think it's actually sunk in yet. I'm just worried about Mom now. How about you?"

"The same. We'll get through it," he replied, putting an arm around his sister's shoulders as he walked with her to the kitchen. When they reached the kitchen, he saw the counter was covered with dishes full of food.

"More food?"

"Yeah. I don't know where to put it anymore. It's nice to have for guests—if Mom was accepting visitors, that is, but she's not. I thought I might start to fill Tupperware containers to freeze the food and return the dishes to the people who brought them. That way, the food won't go bad, and Mom will have food ready when she does start to eat."

"Good idea," Mark said. He then thought to himself, It will also help keep you busy and focused on something besides the issue at hand—something I could use myself. "I'm just going to look in on Mom."

"Oh, by the way," he added, handing her a newspaper, "I picked up today's paper. It should have Dad's obituary in it."

Mark looked in on his mother. She appeared to be sleeping, but Mark wasn't completely convinced. At least she's lying down, he thought.

When he returned to the kitchen, the first thing he noticed was the look on his sister's face. Jan had her hand over her mouth, and a tear trickled down her cheek. The obituary had obviously touched the last raw nerve she had left.

As he put his arm around her, she looked up at him. "Oh, Mark. Remember Mom said that Pat McDermott was supposed to come over on the morning of the accident? Mom couldn't figure out why she hadn't shown up. When we tried to reach her at the office, there was no answer, so we left a message." She paused a second. "I know why we haven't heard from her."

Mark gave Jan a puzzled look. "Yeah?"

"Look at this," she said, and she handed him the paper while pointing to an obituary that was not their father's.

Mark read, and as he did, his grip on his sister tightened.

"Oh my God. Do you think Mom knows?"

"I don't think so."

"Maybe we shouldn't tell her."

"Mark, she's going to find out. Pat was their financial planner, and Mom will want to talk to her about . . . stuff."

"Maybe it's a coincidence. Maybe it's a different accident."

"Mark, she was on her way here. It's got to be the other car involved in Dad's accident. If you want to be sure, why don't you phone the police and confirm."

"Oh, man." Mark ran his hand through his hair, exasperated. "What was the officer's name?"

"Everything is written down beside the phone." Jan ruffled through the papers with different messages on them.

"Here," she said, handing him one. "This is his name and phone number. Do you want me to pour you a coffee while you phone?"

"I'd rather pour the coffee and have someone else phone."

Jan sighed. "Do you want me to call?"

"No, I just wish neither of us had to. You go pour the coffee."

Jan took some salmon sandwiches from a container in the fridge and placed them on two small plates. Then she poured two coffees, grabbed two napkins, and placed everything on the kitchen table.

She had just taken a bite from her sandwich when Mark entered the room and sat across from her. It was apparent from the look on his face that the officer had confirmed their suspicions.

"She was in the other car, wasn't she?"

"I'm afraid so. I still don't know how we're going to tell Mom."

"Tell Mom what?" came a voice from the kitchen doorway. Jan and Mark looked at each other. Neither one had heard her enter the room.

Mark did the talking. "Sit down, Mom. Do you want a sandwich or coffee?"

"What are you so afraid to tell me, Mark?" she asked, ignoring his question.

"Mom, you know there was another car in the accident, don't you?"

Nina hesitated. "Yes," she finally said.

"Mom, the driver of the other car was Pat McDermott."

"Oh my God. How...Oh my God, no. How do you know? Are you sure?"

"Her obituary is in today's paper, and I just phoned the police to confirm. They said it was the same accident."

"Where's the paper? Let me see."

Jan reached over and gave her mother the paper. Nina, who had not read her husband's obituary in the paper yet, went straight to Pat's. As she read, she shook her head.

"Oh, dear God. Her poor children." Nina looked up at her own children. "She talked of them often. They were her pride and joy. I'm not sure, but I believe they are both under 10 years old. Those poor children," she said again as she continued to shake her head.

"It says here that the funeral is Wednesday morning at 10:30. I think we should go."

"Are you sure, Mom?"

"I'm sure. You two didn't know her, but your father and I did. I have to go." Nina put her head down, cupping it with her hands.

"Not only did your father and I know her for years, but it was because of . . . my husband . . . that . . ." A sob escaped.

Mark knew his mother well enough to know that she was thinking of the young woman whose life had been cut short. She would never see her children grow up and those poor children would now grow up without a mother.

Jan went rushing to her mother's side. "Mom, don't think like that. You know Dad was a careful driver; there has to be a reason—car trouble or something. The mechanic is checking out the car, and we should get the results from the autopsy soon. One of those reports should tell us something."

"What if he was driving too fast because I didn't think he should go? What if all of this is my fault? What if both your father and Pat are dead because I was worried that he might be late for some damn appointment?"

"Mom," Mark said, trying to calm his mother down. "You could get Dad to do a lot of things, but to drive stupid or too fast—no one could get him to do that."

"Well, that doesn't change anything does it?" she snapped, obviously regretting it immediately after. "I'm sorry," she said. Her children were doing everything in their power to support her, even while they were dealing with their own loss, and now she was snapping at them.

"I'm so sorry. I'm not dealing with anything very well, am I? For whatever reason it happened, it doesn't change the fact that it did happen," she said with controlled calmness. "I have to go to the funeral. I would appreciate it if you both came with me, but I'd understand if you don't."

Nina rose from the table. "I need to be alone. I think I'll go lie down again," she said as she headed for her bedroom.

Mark knew from the tone in her voice that it was not a time to argue. That tone meant that her mind was made up and no one—not even their father—dared discuss the matter at hand any further. They knew that, with or without them, she was going to Pat McDermott's funeral.

Nina had no sooner entered her bedroom, when she immediately turned around and headed back to the kitchen.

"Mom?" Jan met her at the doorway. "Did you forget something? I can get it for you."

"I need to order flowers for Wednesday."

"I'll do that."

"Thank you, dear, but this is something I need to do."

Wednesday, August 22

NINA ENTERED THE FUNERAL HOME with Mark and Jan on either side of her. The two of them had made a last-minute attempt to change their mother's mind about coming, but it was a losing battle, and they ended up accompanying her instead. Nina was silently relieved; she didn't know if she could handle this alone.

The funeral home was already packed, and every pew was full; the three of them stood in the back against the wall. A few minutes later, someone came by to tell them that there was seating in the next room and that the sermon could be heard over the intercom. Mark tried to guide his mother out of the room.

"Mom, you'll be more comfortable in the other room. You can sit down there." He tried to reason with her, but she wouldn't budge, and the three of them stood in the back.

Nina scanned the room until she found the children who must have been Pat's. Jack sat in the front pew, with Chelsea leaning against his arm and Nathan sitting on his lap. Nathan didn't make a sound, but he was pressed against his father. From the movement of his shoulders, Nina could tell that he was crying. Chelsea's head was resting against her father's other shoulder, and she didn't move.

Nina cried for the small children who would grow up without a mother. At least Mark and Jan were able to become adults before they lost a parent. She fought the urge to go down to where they sat and hold them.

Her line of vision moved beyond the first pew, and she saw that the front of the room was full of flowers. She wondered which of the many bouquets were from her family. Ordering the flowers had been easier than she had thought it would be—until it came time to tell the clerk what to write on the card. Her first instinct had been to say, "Mike and Nina Andrews."

When she realized that she had already signed her last card from Mike and Nina Andrews, the tears welled up, and her chin began to quiver. She paused, took a deep breath to compose herself, and in a whisper said, "Nina Andrews and family." The clerk was very sympathetic, believing the grief only to be because Nina had been very close to the deceased.

Nina looked back to Pat's family. Hadn't Pat mentioned that she and her husband were separated? Had they worked it out? If not, would the children—why couldn't she remember their names?—be moving in with their father now?

She could hear the little boy's cries now as he sat on his father's knee. The little girl still sat quietly, hugging her father's arm. Suddenly, Nina couldn't catch her breath. Panic washed over her, and she felt like she was suffocating. She couldn't stay in the room another moment.

Without saying a word, she turned on her heels and left with more energy and speed than she'd had since the day of the accident. She left the building and went straight to the car, with Mark and Jan close behind her.

As quickly as she had left the room, she stopped in the middle of the parking lot, and the flood of tears began. She cried for Pat and for Mike. She cried for the children they had both left behind. And she cried for herself. The world was an emptier place than it had been only four short days ago.

Mark and Jan both put their arms around her, and the three of them stood huddled together in the parking lot of the funeral home, crying. The only one to speak was Nina, who cried over and over again, "I'm sorry. I'm so sorry."

Mark and Jan never said a word and let her go on until she was too exhausted to cry anymore. When Nina had no more tears to cry, she stepped back, took the last few steps to the car, opened the back door, and got in without saying another word. Jan got in the back seat with her mother, and Mark took the driver's seat. Jan pulled a small water bottle from her purse and a small bottle of the pills the doctor had prescribed for her mother's nerves.

"Here, Mom, take this."

For once, Nina didn't argue. She took the two pills Jan gave her, swallowed them with the help of the water, and wondered how they would get through Friday? Because of the autopsy the police had insisted on, Mike's funeral had been delayed and it was now set for Friday afternoon.

Nina leaned back and closed her eyes. After a few blocks, she sat up, reached for her purse, and took out her cigarettes. Normally, she didn't smoke in the car, especially when Mark and Jan were with her. She knew that they didn't smoke and that it made them uncomfortable in such a small area. Had she thought about it, she wouldn't have lit the cigarette now—but Nina wasn't thinking; she was just doing.

The only thing Nina did know was that the past four days had been difficult and that the next four days weren't going to be any easier. "Lord, give us strength," she silently prayed.

Friday, August 24

EXCEPT FOR THE HUMMING OF the fridge and the muffled sounds of the outside world filtering through, the Andrews home was silent. No one knew what it was that they were supposed to say, so no one spoke a word. The family knew that as difficult as the past six days had been, this was going to be the longest and most difficult day that any of them had ever experienced.

None of them knew just how they were going to manage. They each worried for one another and secretly worried that they would be the one to fall apart, becoming an extra burden for the other two to endure. One thing they did know was that they would not go through this day alone, and that alone gave them each a little comfort.

Because the house was so quiet, Jan thought that she was the first one up. As she entered the kitchen, she saw that the coffee-pot was only half full. She wrapped her hands around the pot and could feel that the contents were hot. That told her that her mother was up—and had been up for awhile. She knew that her mother's routine always included making a full pot of coffee first thing in the morning.

She checked her mother's room and saw that the bed was made. Searching the house, she discovered that her mother was nowhere to be found.

It was when Jan was making her way back to the kitchen, that she saw her mother through the patio doors. With an empty coffee cup and dirty ashtray on the small table beside her, Nina was now slumped back in the chair with her eyes closed, the sun shining on her. Jan hoped she was sleeping and left her with her solitude.

Jan decided that the best way for her to cope today was to keep as busy as possible. If she allowed herself to think of what the day held in store for her, she knew that she would be the first one to collapse. She felt a pang of guilt as she realized that she just wanted this day to be over so that she could finally go back home and fall apart, if even for just an hour. She and Mark had agreed that they were here to help their mother cope; they would deal with their own loss later.

Jan went to the fridge and got the bacon and eggs out. She knew they had to eat something and that it could be several hours before they would eat again. Besides, it would give her something to do.

She was getting the frying pan out to start cooking when Mark came into the kitchen. Jan could tell from his tousled hair and the bags under his eyes that last night had been as rough for him as it had been for her.

They acknowledged each other in silence. Mark leaned against the counter watching his sister, but no one spoke a word until Mark noticed that the coffeepot was half empty.

"How long has Mom been up?" he asked.

"I don't know. She was up before me."

"Where is she?"

"On the deck."

Mark poured himself a coffee and left the room. Jan heard the patio door open and close, and then half a minute later, it opened and closed again. Mark walked back into the kitchen.

"She's weeding the flowers," he said.

"Is she okay?"

"I didn't speak with her. In fact, I don't even think she knew I was there. When she wasn't on the deck, I went looking for her. She's got her gardening gloves on, and she's pulling weeds. She didn't seem to be crying or anything, so I thought she might just want to be left alone."

Jan put six strips of bacon in the frying pan. She let out a sigh, and without looking up she asked, "How do you think she'll do today?"

"I don't know. I don't know how *I'm* going to do."

Jan could hear in his voice that he was fighting for control of his emotions. She wanted to say something to him. She wasn't sure what, but hopefully something to let him know that he could lean on her today. Just as she looked up to speak, she saw him leave the room. Maybe they all needed a little solitude right now.

At two o'clock that afternoon, the limousine from the funeral home pulled up in front of the Andrews' home to pick up Nina and her children. There had been very little said by anyone that day, and since Mark had answered the door for the limousine driver, no one had spoken a word. There was only silence as the girls looked for their purses and Mark put on his suit jacket, all three preparing to leave.

At the reception afterwards, Nina could not understand her anger. She had been feeling a lot of different emotions over the past six days, but all she felt now was the anger. Anger towards her well-meaning friends for the stupid questions they asked; anger at herself for not being stronger; anger at herself for being angry.

But most of all, her anger was towards God for allowing this to happen. How could he have allowed these two people to be taken? As far as Nina was concerned, their time here on earth was not done, and yet He allowed this to happen and now she was alone. Two young children were without their mother, because He allowed this to happen.

A young woman Nina had met a few times at Mike's office offered her condolences. When she asked Nina what she planned on doing now, Nina fought the impulse to use sarcasm. *Oh, I don't know. I thought I'd go shopping later and maybe a game of tennis tomorrow. Are you up for it? Or did you mean longer term. I was thinking of a Caribbean vacation this winter.* Instead, in a voice that was barely audible, she simply said, "I don't know."

It was only a few minutes later when Nina was approached again. This time she was asked how long she was going to take off work. She answered to herself, *Oh, I've thought this over very carefully, because I've had a lot of extra time this week, you know. I have decided that eight days is the amount of time I need. What do you think?* Instead, she simply replied, "I don't know."

When asked how she would be able to manage without Mike, she wanted to snap back, *How will Pat McDermott's children manage without their mother?* Instead, she simply replied, "I don't know."

It baffled Nina that people actually thought that she would have answers to these questions. Were they crazy, or was she?

And when well-wishers said, "May God be with you," she cringed and wanted to say, "Where was God when this accident happened in the first place?" Instead, she simply said, "Thank you."

Afraid of not being able to control her impulses any longer, she made her way outside and found a bench amongst a garden of flowers. There she sat and lit a cigarette.

It was a warm summer day, and she was able to sit outside in comfort. The sun shone down, but the gentle breeze kept Nina from getting too warm in her black jacket.

She studied the different flowers surrounding her and tried to identify each one. By the time Mark found her, she had recognized the roses, snapdragons, day lilies, and petunias. The sound of his voice brought her back to the present, and she realized that she hadn't been thinking of Mike, Pat, or anything to do with the matter at hand; it seemed strange to her.

"Mom, are you okay?"

Nina looked up at her handsome son. He had been such help during this time. Both of her children had. She patted the seat next to her. "Sit down beside me, Dear."

Mark sat down as he was told and repeated his question, "Are you okay?"

"I don't know," she answered honestly without the anger. "I just needed to get away. You know."

"I know," he said, and then hesitated before saying, "Did you want to be alone?"

She reached over and held his hand, "No. It's nice to have you here."

They sat in silence a few moments before Nina said, "I'm sorry I haven't been much help. Sometimes I forget that I am the parent and that I am not the only one grieving. Are you okay?"

"Don't worry about me."

"But that's a mother's job."

Nina noticed that her motherly concern hit him hard, because tears welled in his eyes. "You've always done a good job, Mom—both you and Dad. I'm going to miss him," he said, as his voice quivered.

Nina reached over and wiped his tears away, just as she had done when he was a little boy. "I know you will, Baby. He'd be very proud of the way you're handling everything. He's always been proud of both you and Jan. We both have."

Mark reached out and hugged his mother. Nina hugged him back and then sat back and patted her son's hand.

"Well, we shouldn't leave Jan alone to handle things." With that they returned, Nina's arm linked with her son's. Both had found the strength to face the crowd for another hour.

Wednesday, August 29

JAN AND NINA SAT AT the kitchen table, each with their coffee, and Nina with her cigarette. They were discussing the autopsy.

"A stroke," Nina said for the third time, and she shook her head. "I don't understand it. How can he be fine one minute and dead the next? Shouldn't there have been any symptoms? He was fine."

"When was the last time Dad had a check-up?" Jan asked.

"Oh, I don't know . . . awhile ago, but he was fine."

Jan didn't say what she was thinking, but she didn't have to; Nina was thinking the same thing. The only difference was that Nina voiced it.

"Do you think that if your father had gone to the doctor, he might still be alive—and those children might still have a mother?"

Just then the phone rang, and Jan jumped up to get it. She was relieved that she didn't have to answer the question. A few minutes later, she returned with the phone still in hand. Cupping her hand over the speaker, she whispered, "Mom, it's Georgia. Did you want to talk to her?"

Jan knew that her mother was declining phone calls and visitors, and Jan had become an expert at coming up with excuses. She was prepared to tell Georgia that her mother was taking a nap, but Nina surprised her and took the phone.

"Thanks," she said to Jan, and then into the phone she said, "Hi, Georgia." Jan sat drinking her coffee, listening to one side of the conversation.

"Yeah."

"Sunday night."

"Next Sunday."

From Nina's responses, Jan figured that Georgia had asked when Mark had gone home and when she would be leaving.

"We were just talking about it."

That would be the autopsy, Jan thought.

"It doesn't make sense—at least not to me."

That would be the stroke.

"I hadn't thought of that. Maybe you're right. Maybe I should."

Jan made a mental note to ask her mother what that was about after she hung up.

"I don't know. Where? I don't know if I'm ready. Hang on. Jan?"

Jan had been so busy trying to figure out the one-sided conversation that she hadn't noticed her mother holding the phone for her to take.

"Georgia wants to talk to you."

"Hello?"

When Jan took the phone, Nina grabbed both their cups and went for refills.

When she came back, Jan had hung up.

"So, what did Georgia want to talk to you about?" Nina asked.

"She wanted to know what time I was leaving on Sunday. It sounds like she wants to stop by, so I told her she may as well stay for supper."

Now it was Jan's turn to ask a question. "What did she ask you that you don't think you're ready for?"

"Oh, she wanted to go out for coffee. Honey, do you mind if I go lay down for awhile?"

~ ~ ~ ~ ~ ~ ~ ~ ~ ~ ~ ~ ~ ~ ~ ~ ~ ~ ~

Jack hung his clothes in the closet as he unpacked his bag. The basement was full of his possessions that he couldn't decide what to do with yet. He knew there were still a lot of decisions to make, but some of the decisions could wait; there would be time later.

The landlord had been good enough to let him out of his lease after he heard the circumstances.

"You go take care of your children; they need you now. I won't have any trouble renting your apartment out."

He had been right. The apartment rented out the same day Jack gave his notice, but the new renters wanted to know if they could move in a couple of days early. Because the landlord had been so accommodating, and Jack was lucky enough to find a mover that was available right away, most of Jack's things had already been moved back into his old home. There was no room for his furniture, so that had been put into storage until Jack could decide what to do with it.

As Jack hung another hanger, he realized that it was a tighter squeeze than it used to be. Studying the space that was taken from Pat's clothes, he realized that she had expanded her wardrobe since he left. He grabbed a few of the hangers holding her outfits to make the extra room he needed, and then suddenly he stopped before the hanger even left the rod.

Somehow, by removing her clothes, he felt like he was removing her, and he wasn't ready to do that just yet. Even though they had been in the middle of a divorce, he had never planned on removing her totally from his life.

Besides, wasn't it too early to remove things for Chelsea and Nathan's sake? Jack sat on the bed and thought again of what this meant to Chelsea and Nathan. Was he prepared to help them through this? What did he know about a child's emotions? They had fun with their father, and he had always made sure that they got everything they needed, but when it came to helping them through difficult times, it was their mother who always knew what to do and what to say. Jack felt helpless. He didn't want to let them or Pat down—he had already done enough of that.

"Daddy."

Jack looked up to see Chelsea standing in the doorway. She walked up to where he was sitting and, with her little fingers, she wiped away his tears. "It's okay to cry, Daddy. Mommy used to say that feeling sad was like a pot of rice. If you keep the lid on too tight, it will boil over and get messy. If you keep the sad in, then you will boil over and get messy, so you have to cry and let the sad out."

Jack laughed and held his daughter tight. None of this made any sense to Jack, but it seemed to make perfect sense to her. He looked down at her innocent face and smiled.

"Mommy would say something like that."

"Daddy?"

Chelsea looked like she was carrying the weight of the world on her little shoulders. It broke Jack's heart to see so much pain in one so young. "Yes, Pumpkin?"

"Am I bad if I want to go to school?"

"Bad? No, Sweetheart, why would you say that?"

"Chrissie, next door, said her mommy told her that I probably won't go to school now because my mommy's dead." She started to cry. "I miss Mommy, Daddy. I don't want her to be dead, but I don't want to just stay in my room forever. Am I bad?"

"Oh, Honey, you don't have to stay in your room forever. Mommy would want you to go to school. In fact, why don't the three of us go out this afternoon and buy you some new school clothes and have an ice cream cone."

Chelsea just nodded with cheeks wet from tears.

"Come on," Jack said. "Let's wash your face and get your brother. I can finish unpacking later."

Sunday, September 2

MARK AND JAN HAD BOTH gone home, and Nina was left alone. Her only visitor that day was Georgia, who had stopped by late in the afternoon to check up on her. Nina knew everyone was concerned about her being alone, but she'd had enough of people. She didn't want to see anyone or talk to anyone. Nina fed Georgia some of the food that Jan had taken from the freezer, and then, as gently as she could, she asked her to leave, convincing her that she really just wanted to be alone.

It wasn't long after she left that Carrie phoned. Nina realized that because Carrie lived next door, she had seen Georgia's car drive away, and because she cared, she had called over to make sure that Nina was okay. It took several minutes, but after convincing Carrie that she was fine and really needed a few hours alone, Carrie hung up—but not until Nina promised to phone if she needed anything at all, even if it was the middle of the night. Nina promised, if for no other reason than to get her off the phone.

With everyone convinced that she was fine and that she really did want to be alone, Nina wished she had someone with her. She no longer wanted to be alone with her thoughts. Suddenly the silence was deafening and the house was suffocating. She aimlessly roamed the house, unconsciously looking for any resemblance of life.

When she got to the kitchen, she poured some red wine into a glass, put the bottle back in its place, and took a sip. If she didn't know what to do with a day or an evening, what was she going to do with the rest of her life? If she couldn't cope with this, how did she expect Pat's children to cope?

With that thought, guilt took the place of her self-pity. Nina emptied her glass, grabbed the bottle, and started to pour another. Just as the liquid was about to start coming out of the bottle, she tipped it upright and corked it. She went to the liquor cabinet and traded her bottle of red wine for the bottle of scotch. Sitting back down with her glass of scotch, she lit a cigarette and took a bigger sip than she was used to.

"Whoa. That's a better medicine than wine," she said to an empty room.

Nina thought of the autopsy, and more tears came. She emptied her glass and poured another.

"A stroke," she said aloud.

After a glass of wine and two scotches in a 40-minute period, Nina realized that she had started speaking her thoughts out loud, even though there was no one there to hear them. But speaking aloud made her feel less alone.

"I think I can't hear my thoughts," she said, feeling that she had to justify her action, if only to herself. "They're too scattered. Maybe there are too many. That could be. All those thoughts are going on at the same time, and so I can't hear just one of them."

Getting back to the thought of the moment, she continued. "Anyway, the autopsy said it was a stroke, and they didn't even see it coming. Just like Pat hadn't seen Mike's car coming."

Two days earlier, Nina had met with their family doctor. Normally it took six weeks to get an appointment, but a half-hour opening had been made for her immediately. She wanted to discuss the autopsy. What could they have done to change this? Should they have seen it coming? If she could erase time and go back a couple of weeks or months, would the ending be any different?

Nina wanted desperately to know the answers, but secretly she knew that she was also afraid of the answers. What if this could have been avoided? None of them could change what was done. What would she do with the answers? How could she live without knowing?

The doctor sat patiently, listened to the questions, and then answered each of them. Nina tried to pay very close attention, but now she remembered very little of what she had just been told.

"Why can't I remember anything the doctor said?" Nina asked as she emptied the contents from her glass one more time. Feeling the sensation of the alcohol, she remembered the two small children clinging to their father in the funeral home. A stroke. Their mother was dead because my husband had a stroke.

"So, tell me, God," she said aloud, "what happened? Did you make a mistake?"

Filling her glass again, she realized just how much the drink had taken effect. "Good. I want to feel its effect, cause you know what, God," she said, looking upwards, "it's a whole lot better than what I've been feeling."

Nina stood and held her glass up high above her head, and she was about to make the toast to the heavens, but then she changed her mind. Instead she just lowered her glass and took another drink.

Sitting back down, she repeated, "So, tell me, God, did You make a mistake? And tell me this: When You do make a mistake, do You let anyone know? Do You even admit it?"

Feeling restless, Nina stood again and started to pace. "If You, the almighty God, makes a mistake, how would anyone know? They just say, "Oh, it was God's will. Only He knows what His reasons are. Well, I'm not buying that, God. If You have Your reasons, I want to know what they are."

Nina leaned over to light a cigarette and felt dizzy. "Okay, maybe I'd better sit down again. You know, God, You're not going to get off that easy this time. It's only You and me here, and I want to know. Did You screw up?

"I know, I know. The one thing I do remember the doctor saying is that Mike's stress and smoking probably had a lot to do with the stroke. I don't completely buy that, because how many people have lived the same kind of life that he did, and they're still around?"

Nina shook her head. "No sir, I don't completely buy that."

She paused for a moment, contemplating Mike's lifestyle before she continued. "Just for argument sake, let's say it's true. Why did You have to take those children's mother away? They didn't live that lifestyle. It's not her fault Mike smoked. It's not their fault Mike lived a life with stress."

Thinking of smoking, Nina looked down and saw that her cigarette sitting in the ashtray had almost burned away. Taking one last drag from it, she put it out.

"Yeah, well thanks for not letting it fall out of the ashtray, start a fire, and kill me."

The realization of what she just suggested set in.

"On second thought, maybe You would have been doing me a favour. Maybe my life is over anyway, so You may as well take my body." She said it sarcastically, but she immediately felt ashamed.

"Okay, maybe that one was uncalled for. I'm sorry.

"Anyway, staying on the subject, why did You kill those children's mother? I really want to know. Mike had only been in the car five minutes. All You had to do was have him have the stroke ten minutes earlier, and that woman would still be alive. Those poor children would still have a mother."

Nina wondered if she was getting through to Him. Was she was making her point? Nina tried to reason her argument with God the way she had reasoned her arguments with Mike over the years.

"You see what I'm getting at, God? You screwed up. Now, between You and me, I want to know what You're going to do about this, or would that be admitting You made a mistake? It's okay to make a mistake, you know. I mean, God or not, it's okay to make a mistake."

Nina sat silently for a few moments, waiting for a response. None came. She listened, but the only sound she heard was a car outside driving down the back lane. After the car went by, there was only silence. She continued to sit and wait for the anticipated response. Soon it became more than she could bear, and she knew that if the silence was to be broken, it would have to be broken by her.

"Well, anyway, I can see You're not going to tell me what I want to know. Will You at least tell me what I'm supposed to do now?"

Yawning, Nina covered her mouth and said, "I'm suddenly very tired, so I'm going to go to bed, and maybe tomorrow, You can let me know what You decided."

Nina rose, and just as she was about to leave the room, she remembered her manners, looked up, and said, "Good-night."

Sunday, January 6

NINA SLOWLY OPENED HER EYES. The daylight entering the room through the window let her know that night had passed. She no longer heard the howling of the wind, and she wondered if the storm had passed.

As she rolled over, she felt the wetness on the pillow from the tears she had cried in her sleep. Bewildered, she wondered what it was that she had dreamed about that made her cry. Was she crying for Mike in her sleep? Why was she thinking about Pat McDermott? Did she dream about her? Flickers of memory seeped in, and she had vague memories of worrying about Pat's children.

Maybe if she washed her face, she'd be able to think more clearly. With a plan in mind, Nina quickly rose with more energy than she felt. She studied her reflection in the mirror above the sink. It was a tear-stained face that stared back, but that had become her normal look.

She was reaching for the washcloth when she heard a noise in the distance. Sure that it was coming from another room in the house, Nina listened carefully. There it was again. It sounded like it came from the kitchen. Had Mark or Jan come home while she was sleeping?

Tiptoeing so as not to make a noise, she listened cautiously, fear setting in with each step. What if it wasn't

Mark or Jan? What if an intruder had come in the house while she was sleeping?

Before leaving the room, she looked around for something that could be used as a weapon. On the dresser was a heavy pewter candlestick. Nina picked it up and held it over her head, ready to protect herself.

Noticing the phone next to the candlestick, she picked it up with her other hand. It might be a good idea to have it with her in case there was a need to dial 911.

As she approached each corner and doorway, she stopped and scanned the room for any unwanted visitor. When she got to the doorway of her kitchen, she saw the back of a man working at the counter.

Crouching down, she debated her options. Should I hit him with the candlestick, call 911, or just run for the back door and hope he doesn't catch me before I can get out? Realizing that there was something familiar about him, Nina stayed frozen to the spot.

"Good morning, Nina," the man said without turning around.

Hearing her name, Nina stood up straight.

"You don't need any weapons, so you can put the candlestick down."

Nina looked down at the candlestick in her hand and then returned her gaze to the man standing in her kitchen. He still hadn't turned around. He may have heard her enter, but how did he know she had anything in her hand, let alone that it was a candlestick?

"I've made some coffee. I know you have a cup first thing in the morning. Would you like some?" he asked.

"Um. Yes, please."

Why was she accepting coffee from this strange man in her kitchen, and why wasn't she afraid?

"You know, the good thing about you coming out with a candlestick, ready to protect yourself, is that it shows you have a will to live. I didn't see any of that will last night."

Turning around, he handed her a coffee. Nina noticed that he had put cream in it without asking her. How did he know she didn't take it black? As she took the cup, she studied his face. He looked so familiar. What was his name again?

"Matt."

What did he say? "Sorry?"

"Matt. The name you know me by is Matt. Your mind hasn't completely let go of the events as you last saw them—the way they would have played out. In that scenario, you never met me. It will only take a couple minutes for you to get your thoughts together."

He turned back to the kitchen counter, broke a couple eggs into a bowl, and started to whip them while he continued to explain.

"Soon you'll remember things as they actually happened, not as they would have happened without God's intervention.

"Why don't you sit down at the table and have your coffee? Take a minute to think about it, while I finish making you breakfast just like Mike used to. After you eat, we'll talk."

Obeying, Nina silently walked through the kitchen to take her place at the table. It was when she started to put her coffee down on the table that she saw them. The pills she had intended to swallow to end her life were all lined up perfectly on the table where she normally sat.

She held her cup in midair. Looking from the table to the man in her kitchen, she tried to make sense of what was going on.

"I'm here to help you, Nina," Matt said. "I would like to have thrown those out, but as I told you last night, there are some things that only you can do for yourself. I originally put them in the medicine cabinet so they didn't distract you while we talked, but they are back where you last left them. You are the only one who can permanently remove them."

Nina sat at the kitchen table with her hands wrapped around her coffee cup. She stared at the pills in front of her. Events started scrambling through her mind like a reel on fast forward, but it was like watching two movies at the same time. She was confused; nothing made sense.

Mike was dead, she knew that, but had she called an ambulance to come and get him, or did he die in an accident? Was Pat involved? She remembered talking to her just a few days ago—or did she?

She looked up and saw Matt leaning against the doorway, arms crossed, watching her.

"It's confusing, isn't it, Nina?" He brought her breakfast over and sat at the chair next to her.

"What happened?" she asked.

"You've been given a very rare opportunity, Nina. A gift, really."

"I remember a lot of different things, but I don't know what the truth is."

"In a way, they both are. You've been very angry because you think God made a mistake. You think that everything that happened is because God did nothing. This anger you felt was not only holding you back; it was destructive.

"God *did* do something, Nina. Mike created his own ending, just as most humans do. And just as most humans do, when the ending wasn't what you wanted, you blamed God.

"Mike did have a stroke in the yard, and you did phone the ambulance. Pat is at home with her children, and she has a very good life in front of her."

Matt sat silently for a moment, knowing this was not easy for her. She was remembering the circumstances around Mike's death both ways—the way they happened and the way they would have happened, had God not intervened. It was difficult for her to keep them straight and to know which was true.

"God has given humankind choice. People choose how they want to live their lives, whether they want to help others or hurt them, whether they want to find good in the world or evil, and whether they want to live a healthy lifestyle or not. Mike was a good man and he had a happy life, but it was his choice to live the lifestyle that he did. It was many of his choices that shortened his life. His choices and his choices alone, Nina. Humankind must learn to take responsibility for their decisions.

"God didn't shorten Mike's life, and God didn't make a mistake. Mike had a hand in his death. It was because of Mike's own doing that he had the stroke. What God did was change where and when Mike had the stroke. By doing that, he changed the outcome of what would have been."

Matt paused to give Nina time to take it in. Then he said, "You've seen both. You've seen what would have been and what is."

A tear fell down Nina's cheek as she listened.

"Pat is still alive. Chelsea and Nathan still have a mother. That was God's hand. When He performs a miracle, He doesn't announce it to the world for their gratitude."

Matt saw that Nina was still trying to take all the information in, but couldn't quite grasp the concept of what had happened yet. God had performed a miracle, and she had been allowed to see it. Matt knew that God had not shown her the miracle for her gratitude, but rather to help her through this time.

"Nina, when you do something to help Mark or Jan, do you do it for their gratitude? Do they know every time you have helped them?"

Nina thought back to the different times that Mike and she had helped one of their children and then agreed not to say anything. They hadn't expected gratitude, because oftentimes Mark and Jan never even knew that Mike and Nina had stepped in. All they had wanted was to make it a little easier for their children.

"God has blessed you, your children, and Pat and her family. Mark and Jan have already lost one parent, Nina. Don't make them lose another. Before I arrived last night, you were on the road to destruction. Your children would have lost another parent, and because you chose to end the life God has given you, you would have lived eternally without seeing Mike again. That would have been your hell.

"What you saw last night were the events as they would have happened. The memories you have of Mike having the stroke in the backyard are the events as He changed them, and those are the memories you will keep. Your spirit will know both scenarios, and this will help you accept your life as it is now, but you will have no memories of the accident or me.

"If you don't think you'll be needing those anymore," Matt said as he pointed to the pills, "why don't you take those away while I pour you another coffee? You've let this one get cold."

Nina nodded. Slowly she gathered up the pills and started down the hall. She knew she had more questions to ask him and wanted to hurry back. Quickly flushing the pills down the toilet, she turned straight around, making her way back to the kitchen. When she didn't see him, she called his name.

"Matt. Matt?"

She listened, but there was no response, only silence. I never heard him leave, so he must be here, she reasoned. Otherwise, I would have heard the door. Besides, he didn't have time to leave. I was only gone a matter of seconds.

Nina picked up her coffee cup that was on the table and wrapped her hands around it. She was aware of the fact that it was freshly poured, because the cup was warm to the touch from the hot liquid inside. As Nina held the cup, she looked around. She was alone. The ringing of the phone made her jump, but she managed to keep the coffee from spilling out of the cup.

"Mom? I didn't wake you, did I?"

Nina recognized her daughter's voice immediately. "Not at all," she said. "I was just about to have a coffee, so the timing is perfect. How are you?"

"Fine. You sound good," Jan replied.

"You know," Nina said, "I feel good. I don't know what it is, but for some reason I feel like a weight has been lifted off my shoulders. I must have got a good night sleep last night, because I really don't remember the last time I looked forward to the day.

"The storm has lifted," she continued, looking out the window, "and it actually looks beautiful outside."

"So, what have you got planned for the day?" Jan asked her mother.

"I think I deserve a massage. Why don't you come home, spend the night, and phone in sick tomorrow, play hooky. You can join me for a massage, and then we'll order in Chinese food and rent a movie."

Jan laughed. "I'd love to Mom, but I can't. You go ahead and have a massage today, and then maybe the next time I'm down, we'll get a complete makeover. You know, massage, facial, new hairdo—the whole works. Maybe we'll each get ourselves a new outfit and go out for supper too."

"You're on," Nina said, laughing.

Hanging up the phone a few minutes later, Nina started to tidy up when the phone rang again.

"Hello?"

"Nina, this is Pat McDermott. How are you?"

For some reason that Nina didn't understand, the sound of Pat's voice lifted her spirits a little more. Why did she have a feeling of relief? That something that had gone wrong was now right?

"Pat. I'm fine. How are you?"

"I'm great, actually. I just phoned to confirm our appointment for tomorrow. We made a lot of decisions over the past few months, and I just wanted to make sure you were still comfortable with them."

"Great," Nina said. "That's 1:30 tomorrow afternoon, right?"

"Yes, it is."

"Okay, I'll see you tomorrow."

Nina noticed that Pat paused for a moment before continuing, "By the way, I wasn't going to say anything until tomorrow when I could show my ring off, but I'm too happy not to say anything. I'm getting married."

"Congratulations. I'm so happy for you. What's his name?"

"Gordon. We've been seeing each other since last summer, and the kids love him."

"Well, make sure you have an extra few minutes tomorrow to tell me all about him."

"I will. See you tomorrow," Pat said, and they hung up.

Later, as Nina undressed for the shower, a glitter caught her eye. There, in the basket where she kept her makeup, was a necklace hanging over a crumpled picture. She lifted the necklace and studied the pendant as she held it in the palm of her hand. The pendant was a golden globe. It looked vaguely familiar, but she couldn't remember when or where she got it.

Somehow, she just knew there was a connection between this necklace and Mike. It was the type of necklace that Mike would have given her, but he couldn't have, or she would have remembered that. Why couldn't she remember?

Picking up the picture, she recognized it as the picture of her and Mike taken in front of their motor home just before they left for their road trip last summer.

She silently wished he were there to share new experiences with her, but she knew it would never be. Studying the necklace, she wondered if a trip would do her some good. She'd always wanted to take a cruise. She could use a change, and it would give her a break from the winter. She decided to give Georgia a call later and see if she was interested.

She knew that Mike had understood and shared her passion for travel. Maybe I'll stop by a travel agent this afternoon, and tomorrow when Pat gets here, I'll talk to her about building some travel money into the budget, she thought.

Hanging the necklace around her neck, she turned and stepped into the shower. It was time to get on with her day.

Look for

JUNE MCCULLOUGH'S

next novel
coming soon

HOME TO STAY

Turn the page for a preview

Chapter One

As DIANA MANEUVERED HER CAR through the traffic on Highway #1, she passed the Canada Olympic Park to her right and knew her turnoff was not much further. From here, traffic permitting, she would be home within the half-hour. Although she had never stopped referring to Aces Corral as her home, it was two years since she had last been there. She made her turn onto Sarcee Trail and felt the butterflies in her stomach come to life.

It had been an impulse to leave—no, not an impulse, she corrected herself, more of an abrupt necessity. The decision to leave had been a quick decision, but she knew that, had she stayed, she wouldn't have survived.

The decision to come home had been just as abrupt. She supposed that the thought had been brewing in the back of her mind for some time, but last week she suddenly awoke one morning with the decision instantly made. She was going home.

She made the turn from Sarcee Trail onto Bow Trail, but it wasn't until she turned onto the Old Banff Coach Road, driving through the area known as Coach Hill, that she felt her throat tighten. Easy girl, she told herself. You've covered a lot of distance today; just hang on a little longer.

When Diana was a young girl, the West Springs subdivision had not existed. Not yet a part of the city of Calgary, this area had consisted only of farms and acreages. Now, the open pastures and cropland of her youth had been converted into crowded urban lots on both sides of the road.

She felt a sense of loss as she remembered what her father had always said, "I will never move to the city, but if we stay here long enough, the city will move to us." As a child of ten, she hadn't understood his logic, but now as a woman of twenty-five, she saw that his prediction was coming true. She looked around and realized that the city was even closer to the ranch than the last time she traveled this road. The question was—how much closer?

Moments later, she felt a rush of relief as her question was answered. As the subdivision ended, the scenery suddenly changed to the one she remembered. She was delighted to know that the city had not migrated to them yet. From here, she knew, it was another ten minute drive.

Known as the foothills, this area was nestled between the prairies and the Rocky Mountains. You could see the land stretch for miles with an outline of the mountains as the background in the distance. The only obstruction of the view was the clusters of trees and perhaps a house every mile or so. This was good land—useful land—land where a person could make their living by growing a crop or raising livestock.

Although she appreciated the beauty of the towering mountains of British Columbia, with their snow-topped peaks year round, she never got over the feeling of being closed in while she was there. But this—this was the land she had grown up with and loved.

The trees she passed had an outline of green from the buds, which would soon turn to leaves. Although the spring air was still crisp, the bright noon sun shining through the windshield would have made the car uncomfortably warm, had Diana not had the cool air from the air conditioner gently blowing on her.

Noticing the Douglas' house to her right, she knew it was only a matter of minutes before she would reach her destination. Diana pulled the car over to the shoulder of the road and out of the way of any traffic. Shifting the car into PARK, she turned off the ignition and stepped out. As she leaned against the front of the car, she took a cigarette from the package and placed it between her lips.

She noticed her hand shake as she held the flame from the lighter to the cigarette. The butterflies began fluttering again and she held her hand against her stomach to calm them.

Smoking was a habit she had given up the year before, but since making the decision to return, her nerves had started to become unraveled and she had picked up the habit once again. I know this is what I want, she thought, while looking around. It's time to come home and stop running. I know I'm doing the right thing. So why am I so nervous?

Two years earlier, as Diana had packed her suitcases to leave, she knew she couldn't stay. Now, she only knew she could no longer stay away.

"Excuse me."

Broken from her thoughts, Diana looked up to see an older half ton truck, with signs of rust on the door, stopped beside her. The window was rolled down and a man Diana guessed to be about fifty was watching her.

"Need any help?"

"No thanks. I just stopped to stretch my legs."

With that, the gentleman gave a wave of his hand as he stepped on the gas pedal and moved on. Before anyone else could stop to offer help to what appeared to be a stranded motorist, Diana put her cigarette out and got back in her car to finish her journey.

It was only a matter of minutes before she saw the driveway, slowed the car down and turned in. It was a long driveway, which curved around a mixture of poplar and spruce trees. A month from now, when the leaves had filled out, the trees would keep the house completely hidden from the road.

When the ranch-style bungalow was in sight, she saw two men loading an object onto a truck. As she got closer, she realized it was the dining room suite that had stood in her parents' dining room for as far back as she could remember.

With a twist of the wrist, she pulled up in front of the garage door, stopped the motor and turned to pick her purse up from the front passenger seat. As she was putting the car keys into her purse, she heard the car door open.